8674

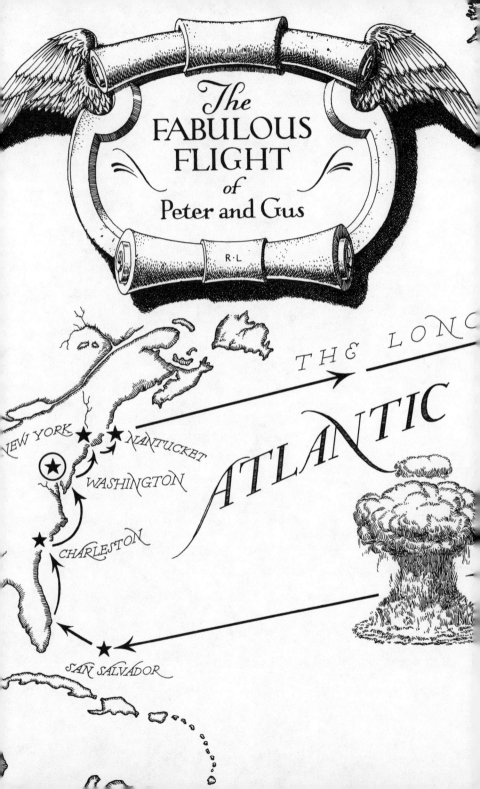

The Fabulous Flight

The Fabulous Flight

by ROBERT LAWSON

ILLUSTRATED BY THE AUTHOR

Little, Brown and Company
Boston   Toronto   London

Library of Congress Cataloging in Publication Data

Lawson, Robert, 1892–1957.
   The fabulous flight.

   Reprint. Originally published: Boston: Little,
Brown, 1949.
   Summary: Peter Peabody Pepperell, who has shrunk to
a tiny size, takes off on an adventure on the back of his
seagull friend Gus.
   1. Children's stories, American. [1. Adventure and
adventurers — Fiction. 2. Size — Fiction. 3. Gulls —
Fiction] I. Title.
PZ7.L4384Fab 1984   [Fic]   84-14419
ISBN 0-316-51731-3 (pbk.)

10 9 8 7 6 5 4 3 2

RRD VA

Published simultaneously in Canada
by Little, Brown & Company (Canada) Limited

PRINTED IN THE UNITED STATES OF AMERICA

Contents

The Fabulous Flight

CHAPTER 1

Peter

Until he reached the age of seven Peter Peabody Pepperell III was a perfectly normal child. In fact he was a little brighter than the average and perhaps a trifle larger.

But shortly after his seventh birthday, for no reason that anyone could discover, he suddenly stopped growing. It was quite puzzling, for his health was excellent, he was active, energetic and had the usual ferocious appetite that goes with that age. It was puzzling to his parents, but not especially alarming. Each day his mother weighed and measured him, but for several weeks both height and weight remained stationary.

"Just a temporary phase," his father guessed. "He has been growing quite rapidly and now there has to be a slight pause while the rest of his system catches up. These fluctuations in the growth rate are noticeable in all Nature; trees, flowers, vegetables and so forth. They are especially pronounced in the marine crustacea."

"What are they?" Peter asked.

"Clams, crabs, oysters, lobsters, crawfish, barnacles, mussels, coral polyps — there are a great many."

"I'd like to be a crawfish," Peter said, "they can run backwards as fast as anything." He demonstrated the locomotion of a crawfish, knocking over the small table which bore his mother's cherished crab-claw cactus.

"Suppose you try imitating a barnacle," Mr. Pepperell suggested, "or perhaps a coral polyp."

This lack of growth was merely puzzling, but when Peter did again begin to grow his parents really became upset. For he began to grow smaller!

At first his mother could not believe it, but after several successive measurements proved that he had grown almost three-eighths of an inch shorter, with a corresponding decrease in weight, both parents decided that Dr. Chutney should be consulted at once.

Dr. Chutney had taken care of Peter Peabody ever since

he was born, in fact for some time before. He knew Mr. and Mrs. Pepperell very well indeed. So well that he didn't pay much attention when Mrs. Pepperell told him of their problem.

"All right, all right, Mary," he said. "Mustn't get excited, mustn't get excited. Everyone's liable to make a mistake, but we'll look at him if it'll make you feel better."

"I feel perfectly all right," Mrs. Pepperell answered, "and I haven't made any mistake. Measure him yourself and weigh him yourself and write it down — and paste it in your hat. I *know* I'm right."

So with much jocularity Dr. Chutney weighed and measured Peter, wrote down all the figures on a little blue card and put it in a filing cabinet. He scratched a prescription and gave it to Mrs. Pepperell.

"A teaspoonful after each meal," he said. "Just a little tonic. Bring him around again in a couple of weeks. Goodby Peter, and don't grow down any more — *grow up.* Ha, ha."

"I wish *you* would," Mrs. Pepperell said.

She brought Peter Peabody back at the end of two weeks and after Dr. Chutney had weighed and measured him he looked greatly puzzled. He got out the little blue card with the last measurements, studied it and looked still more puzzled.

"It's impossible, Mary," he finally said, "quite impossible, but you seem to be right."

"I don't see why that's so impossible," she replied, quite sharply.

"I mean about Peter," he said. "There *does* appear to be a positive decrease in height and weight. We'll have to look into this."

For ten days or so Dr. Chutney looked into it, and into Peter Peabody, with fluoroscopes, bronchoscopes, X rays, microscopes, cardiographs and all sorts of things. Peter Peabody didn't mind especially, because none of it hurt, but it *was* a bit tiresome. At the end of this period Peter had grown a quarter of an inch shorter and Dr. Chutney had to admit himself stumped.

"I can't understand it, Mary," he confessed. "It's completely beyond me. Obviously a disturbance of the sacro-pitulian-phalangic gland (we call it *sac-pit* for short) but whether a recession, a degeneration, or a reversal I am not prepared to say."

"What would that mean — in English?" Mrs. Pepperell asked.

"Well, it's this way. The sacro-pitulian-phalangic gland regulates the growth of the human body. Ordinarily it ceases to function about the age of twenty, when the subject has attained full growth. In rare instances it, the sac-pit, degenerates at a very early age — hence we have dwarfs. In other cases, also rare, it continues to function long after the normal time — then we have giants — "

"I saw a giant at the circus last summer," Peter Peabody

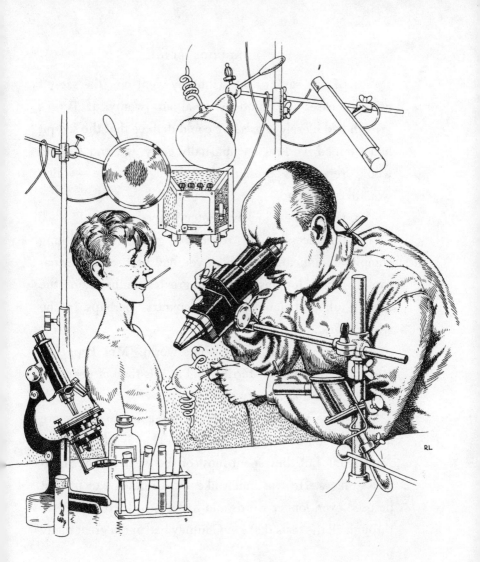

offered. "His name was Wottaman Werner. He shook hands with me and he had pictures of himself with his autograph on them. They cost a quarter and Father wouldn't buy me one. I didn't want it anyway."

"— As I was saying," Dr. Chutney went on, "the sac-pit usually ceases its functions at about twenty. If Peter's growth had merely *ceased* we could deduce that the sac-pit had stopped work at an unusually early age and that he would retain his present size throughout life — which wouldn't be so bad —"

"No, I could be a jockey," Peter Peabody said.

"But this recession, this *reversal* of growth, is something completely unheard of. I think you had best see Dr. Squarosa at Johns Hopkins. He is the greatest authority on the sacro-pitulian-phalangic in this country, perhaps in the whole world."

"I'm not interested in the whole world," Mrs. Pepperell said, "and Baltimore is terribly hot at this time of year, but I suppose we'd better try him."

So in due time she and Peter drove up to Baltimore and spent a week with Aunt Dora. That is, they visited Aunt Dora, but they spent most of the week in Dr. Squarosa's offices. He was much like Dr. Chutney except that he used even longer words and had a beard. He put Peter through all the tests that Dr. Chutney had and a great many more.

Peter rather enjoyed the visit because Aunt Dora always had wonderful food and four ship models that her grandfather had built, but he didn't care much for Dr. Squarosa. Dr. Squarosa wore thick glasses that made his eyes look like owls' eyes and his beard smelled of cigar smoke. At the end of the week the Doctor gave Mrs. Pepperell his pronouncement.

"This, Madam," he said, "is the most remarkable case that I have encountered in forty years of practice. My investigations have convinced me that in this child the functions of the sacro-pitulian-phalangic gland have, in some unaccountable manner, become reversed. In short, instead of causing him to grow larger it is making him smaller. Did he, by any chance, suffer any severe shock, or blow, or accident about the time that this change became noticeable?"

"I fell out of the apple tree last fall," Peter volunteered, "and hit my chest on a rock. It hurt like everything, but Dr. Chutney said it wasn't important."

"He always says everything isn't important," Mrs. Pepperell said.

"This may possibly have been the cause of the trouble," the doctor went on, "it is also possible that a similar fall or blow might restore the gland to its normal functioning."

"But we can't go around throwing Peter out of apple trees or pounding his chest with rocks all the time," Mrs. Pepperell protested. She told Peter to go out and play with the nurse and turned to the doctor again. "Does this mean — an operation?" she asked hesitantly.

"I am afraid an operation is out of the question," Dr. Squarosa answered. "The sac-pit is so closely interconnected with the entire nervous system that any attempt to operate might have disastrous results. It might turn him into a hopeless imbecile — or an interpretive dancer or something."

"Heaven forbid," Mrs. Pepperell exclaimed hastily. "I'm rather relieved though; I hate the idea of operations . . . But Doctor, where will this all end?"

"That is what puzzles me," Dr. Squarosa confessed. "However, things are not as distressing as they might seem. Peter is a fine boy, a bright, healthy child and extremely likeable. His mental development, which is excellent, will continue at the usual rate. He is now seven, so he will be fourteen before his size becomes infinitesimal. In those seven years science may possibly find some solution; I shall work on the problem myself. Or some unforeseen event may cause the gland to resume its normal functions. I shall, of course, keep in close touch with you. Good luck, and don't take it too hard."

Mrs. Pepperell collected Peter, who was practicing first aid by putting a splint on the nurse's left arm, and they went back to Aunt Dora's.

CHAPTER 2

The Workshop

Mr. and Mrs. Pepperell had a long talk about the situation, although there was nothing much they could do about it. Neither was particularly upset. Mrs. Pepperell did feel somewhat disappointed because she had wanted Peter to grow six feet two inches tall and become a General or a Colonel as most of her brothers had.

Mr. Pepperell, however, pointed out that even if Peter had become six feet two he might not have become a General or a Colonel; he might have only been a Major. As Mrs. Pepperell particularly loathed Majors she felt much better about the whole thing.

"And his clothing problem will be so simple," she said cheerfully. "For years I've done nothing but let down trousers and sleeves and let out seams. Now all I have to do is to start taking them in again."

Mr. Pepperell was even more cheery about it. "By George," he laughed, "when he gets *really* small he'll be a great help to me in my work. Lately he's been getting quite large and clumsy, but if he gets smaller and keeps getting brighter it will be wonderful."

What Mr. Pepperell referred to as his "work" was really his hobby. This consisted of making tiny models of every conceivable thing. His actual work was in the State Department in Washington.

In the State Department Mr. Peter P. Pepperell II was a dignified and highly important figure, one of the most important and respected there. But the moment he got home he forgot all about the State Department and usually made a beeline for his workshop.

The workshop occupied the whole of a one-story wing on the north end of the Pepperell home. The house was a big rambling structure out in the country near Washington. At one time this wing had contained a large billiard room, a conservatory and several small rooms. Mr. Pepperell had thrown them all into one huge space and taken it over for his own — and Peter's. At one end was a fireplace surrounded by comfortable, usually dusty, armchairs. On each side of the fireplace were shelves filled with (to a boy) fascinating books.

Along one side of the long room ran a bench that bore an endless array of lathes, drills, grinders, buffers, sanders, routers, buzz saws, band saws and every other sort of machine that one could ever want, as well as a great many that one would never want. Ranged in neat racks and cabinets were ranks and battalions of sharp well-oiled tools. Shelf after shelf was filled with boxes of nails, brads, screws, bolts, nuts and rivets. In what had been the conservatory were a forge and an anvil for metal work. Before a north window stood a drafting table where Mr. Pepperell could plan his various projects.

Once in the workshop, when he had donned a greasy old smock, gotten his hair full of sawdust, his hands covered with oil and a few smudges on his face, Mr. Pepperell lost all resemblance to a high State Department official. He became just an enthusiastic, messy young boy.

Not that he was messy in his work. The models he built were exquisitely accurate and beautifully finished. There were models of all sorts of ships, from Old Ironsides to the latest type of submarine. There were models of naval guns and field guns and siege guns. He built model steam engines, gasoline engines, coaches, carriages, houses, furniture and airplanes. But his greatest pride and Peter's joy was the Pepperell Central Railroad.

This had been under construction for a year or two and had now grown so elaborate that its tracks threatened to usurp the entire workshop, large as it was. There were two terminals, each with a maze of tracks and switches. There were signal towers and a complete electric signal system. There were towns and factories and farms along the right of way. There were water towers, grain elevators and coal elevators. There was a dock with freight sheds, cranes, chutes and tipples. There were tunnels, culverts and crossovers. There were suspension bridges, drawbridges and lift bridges that really worked. As for rolling stock there was every type of locomotive from stubby switch engine to streamlined Diesel, every sort of car from de luxe Pullman to coal-laden gondola.

All this, elaborate though it was, was regarded by Peter and his father as merely a beginning. They were continually planning new expansions and new equipment. Mr. Pepperell drew up plans and consulted a contractor with the purpose of doubling the size of the workshop wing.

It is little wonder that Peter loved his father and this small boy's paradise of a workshop. It is little wonder that Mr. Pepperell loved his son and actually looked forward to his growing smaller and smaller and smarter and smarter.

Peter himself was the least concerned of anyone over this reversal of his growth. Indeed he was quite happy over it. For one thing it got him out of school, which was a great joy.

As he had grown smaller in body his mind seemed to develop even more rapidly than before, so his promotions were regular and frequent. This put him in classes where the other boys were much larger than he and made them appear as rather backward louts, although many of them were not. This, in turn, led to considerable hard feeling, for parents were always saying to their sons, "Why aren't you as smart as that little Pepperell boy? Goodness, he can't be more than half your age." If they protested that he *was*, it was dismissed as nonsense — no one that tiny could possibly be ten or eleven or whatever it happened to be.

To avoid embarrassment all around the Pepperells decided to remove Peter from school and continue his education at home, which suited him perfectly.

A young niece of Mrs. Pepperell's came to live with them and tutored Peter every morning. Barbara was a charming girl who had wanted to be a tap dancer but somehow had gone to college and gotten educated instead. She not only had a brilliant mind and gorgeous blond hair, but was lots of fun as well. So Peter's education progressed rapidly and pleasantly.

"Moreover," Mr. Pepperell pointed out, "he has the great privilege of associating with *me* a large part of the time, an opportunity for which many a young man would cheerfully give his eyeteeth."

"Any young man who wanted to become a mechanic might," Mrs. Pepperell answered. "I had hoped for something higher for Peter."

She spoke rather sharply for she was still a bit nettled over her recent dinner party. A few nights before the Pepperells had entertained several extremely important guests. There were two Justices of the Supreme Court, an Admiral, a General, the Australian Ambassador and, of course, their

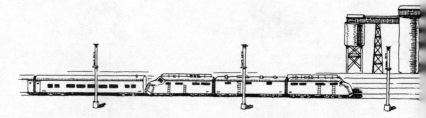

wives. It was all very delightful but, unfortunately, after dinner the gentlemen had retired to the workshop for their coffee and cigars. There they were joined by Peter and there, despite repeated summonses, they had remained the entire evening, shamefully neglecting their social duties — and wives.

The two Supreme Court Justices had an extremely undignified squabble as to which should be chief Train Dispatcher at the Eastern terminus of the Pepperell Central Railroad, a dispute which required all Mr. Pepperell's well-

known diplomatic tact to settle. The Australian Ambassador buried himself in one of the dusty armchairs by the fire with a book on the Flora and Fauna of the Great Barrier Reef and refused to be disturbed.

Mr. Pepperell and the General had a long argument on the correct handling of one of the model cannon, which necessitated firing it off several times. Barbara came in to shoo Peter off to bed, but remained to flirt with the Admiral who, although exactly three times her age and several times a grandfather, always enjoyed that sort of thing. At the moment he was attempting, quite unsuccessfully, to operate a wood lathe. He had cut one thumb and this together with spatters of flying oil had made quite a mess of his full dress uniform. Barbara cleaned him up as well as she could and persuaded him to take on the less dangerous job of chief Signal Operator of the Pepperell Central. It was high time, for the two Justices, through sheer stubbornness and lack of co-operation, had managed to have several bad train wrecks.

Peter acted as General Superintendent and chief trouble shooter, and occasionally as messenger to the pantry to order more refreshments. When it was time for the guests to depart he sat on the Admiral's shoulder while they all sang, "For He's a Jolly Good Fellow."

A grand time was had by all — except Mrs. Pepperell. Spending a long evening with five ill-assorted, uncongenial and impatient wives had been quite a strain and not at all

her idea of a good time. It is not to be wondered at that she was a trifle irritated with the workshop and its attractions, but her irritations never lasted long.

So the months and then the years went happily by, while Peter continued to grow slowly but steadily smaller. This change was so slow and everyone was so used to it that it all seemed perfectly natural and not at all strange to anyone, even when he had become only ten or twelve inches tall. It was only occasionally when Mrs. Pepperell saw a snapshot of Peter when he was his largest that she realized how small he had actually grown. At these times she sometimes sighed slightly, thinking what a handsome Colonel or General he might have made. Then she would realize that after all he might only have been a Major and then she would be happy again.

CHAPTER 3

You're in the Army Now

It was about this time that Peter began getting well ac-
quainted with the small animals. Living in the country as
they did there had always been many squirrels, rabbits,
woodchucks and skunks around the place. Also, though not
so numerous, a few foxes, raccoons, opossums and deer.
Peter liked all these animals and had always tried to make
friends with them, but when he was a large and rather
clumsy boy they had been afraid of him. However, as he
became smaller and smaller they gradually lost their shy-
ness. Now that he was their own size, in fact smaller than
many, they became his closest friends and playmates.

This was most fortunate, for Peter was now far too small to play with other boys, and while his life could not be called at all a lonesome one, still there *were* some pretty long afternoons. Mornings, of course, were occupied by lessons with Barbara; evenings, Saturdays, Sundays and holidays were mostly spent in the workshop with Mr. Pepperell. The afternoons were the only times that were apt to be at all boring. Now all this was changed and the afternoons became almost the happiest and most exciting part of the day.

His special pal was Buck, a big, powerful, rangy rabbit. It was Buck who suggested that Peter ought to take up riding. Mr. Pepperell obligingly manufactured a small Western saddle, complete in every detail. He also made a small pair of cowboy chaps to protect Peter's legs from brush and briars. They were of lovely soft leather and had the monogram P.P.P. III worked in silver wire. No bridle, of course, was necessary; Peter merely guided Buck by pulling the tips of his ears. Besides, Buck went pretty much as he pleased anyway.

Of course it took some time and many falls before Peter learned to ride really well, but soon he developed into a perfect centaur. No jump, no matter how high or how long, disturbed his balance in the least.

Every afternoon, directly after lunch, Buck was waiting out by the terrace. Quickly Peter would saddle up and then they were off. They had glorious rides all over the country-

side. It was a pretty sight to see, for usually they were accompanied by a half dozen of the younger rabbits and were sometimes joined by the fox or the red deer. Up and down hills, across fields and pastures the whole cavalcade would pound, soaring over walls and ditches, circling thickets, Peter's bright neck-handkerchief streaming out behind, as he shrieked and shouted with glee.

One day tragedy almost overtook them. They were returning home after a long run when they were suddenly set upon by a pair of screaming beagles. Ordinarily Buck could have easily outrun them, but in his present tired state and handicapped by Peter's weight, things looked serious. The younger rabbits tried valiantly to distract the hounds, circling and crossing under their very noses, the fox even snapped and snarled at their flanks, but they refused to be diverted. They wanted Buck and he knew it.

Peter, terrified, crouched low and tried to make himself as light as possible, but it was no use; the hounds gained

steadily. Their gaping jaws and lolling tongues were now but a few feet from Buck's laboring flanks.

At this moment Peter realized that the deer was running most peculiarly, his head bent low, his small antlers threatening to interfere with Buck's progress. He was about to shout a warning when the deer snorted, "Grab hold, grab hold."

Then Peter understood. The next time the bobbing antlers came close he rose in the saddle and threw both arms around one tine, at the same time kicking his feet free of the stirrups. For one awful moment it seemed that he would lose his grip, then he managed to swing his legs up and settle tightly into a crotch of the horn. The deer raised his head and set out across the field at a pace that left the yapping hounds far behind. Buck, his load lightened, put on extra speed and gained the shelter of a briar patch. The fox and the younger rabbits scattered in every direction.

They all finally gathered at the terrace. Peter was exhausted from the scare, Buck's sides still heaved and the saddle was all awry. One of the young rabbits had lost a large tuft of fur. Otherwise all were safe.

Mr. Pepperell, when told, looked grave and forbade any further riding until he had taken steps. It happened to be a Friday so he could spend the whole week end in the workshop. On Monday he presented Peter with the result of his labors; two beautifully made little six-shooters, complete with ammunition, belts and holsters. The cartridges were only blanks, but in spite of their small size they made a very impressive bang.

Peter was delighted and Buck couldn't wait to see them put to use. "Come on," he urged, directly after lunch, "let's go get them blasted hounds."

They rode out to the place where the beagles lived and cavorted around until the hounds came bellowing forth. Buck lolloped around most tantalizingly, decoying them over to a hillside pasture where was waiting an enthusiastic audience of young rabbits, as well as the deer and the fox. Then his progress became even more leisurely. The hounds were practically on his heels when Peter, turning in the saddle in best Western style, blazed away directly into their faces with both six-shooters. The hounds slid to a stop, one of them turning two surprised somersaults. With tails between their legs they ran, shrieking, for home.

While Buck and the young rabbits rolled on the ground in glee Peter fired another volley. Then they all returned home in triumph. They never saw the beagles again.

Perhaps it was an inheritance from his mother's Army family which started Peter on training his animal friends in military exercises. The first attempt was made with two miniature field guns, gladly loaned by Mr. Pepperell.

Twelve chipmunks were broken to harness and, six to each gun, drew them with great dash. The gunners were field mice who were taught to sit rigidly upright on the caissons, arms folded on chests, while the guns rattled and bounced over the lawn. The gunners quickly learned to unlimber the guns, load, fire and limber up again with perfect speed and precision. They performed almost every evening for Mr. and Mrs. Pepperell and Barbara, as they had coffee on the terrace. To the army were soon added three supply wagons and two ambulances, all drawn by meadow mice and driven by stolid but very profane hoptoads.

Peter's crowning achievement, however, was the organization and training of the Mephitis Old Guards. With much care and considerable diplomacy he managed to select eight perfectly matched skunks from a great number of eager applicants. These were formed into a squad which was drilled and drilled until their perfection would have

put a West Point drill team to shame. Napoleon watching the march-past of the Old Guard could never have felt his heart swell more proudly than did Peter as, mounted on Buck, he barked out his orders and watched their precise execution.

It was pride of his men, rather than any personal vainglory, which led Peter to plan his GRAND MILITARY EXHIBITION AND DISPLAY. To make it more impressive he decided to keep it a military secret which, as it turned out, was a slight tactical error.

Mr. and Mrs. Pepperell were planning a large garden party and since many of the guests were to be military, Air Force and naval personages it seemed to offer a suitable occasion and a perfect setting.

Peter worked out his plans with the greatest thoroughness and rehearsed his army strictly for many days. He had also organized an Air Force which, although perhaps not quite as well drilled as the ground forces, still could put on an impressive show. At one end of the lawn was a semicircle of evergreens making a stagelike area that was an ideal field for the maneuvers. Behind the screen of evergreens he persuaded Sam, the butler, to place an old phonograph on which was a record of the "Caisson Song."

The exact schedule for G. P. Day (Garden Party Day) was as follows: At X hour + 09 Peter would start the phonograph, mount Buck and take his place at the head of the Mephitis Old Guards, behind evergreens, at center. At X hour + 10, one shot from his six-shooter would be the signal for the two field guns to dash in from left and right, unlimber and fire a salute. Another shot would signal the grand entrance of the Mephitis Old Guards, center. They would be followed by the wagon train and two ambulances. After these had ranged themselves in the background the Mephitis Guards would perform their drill. When that was completed another salute from the guns would start the Aerial Review.

Three squadrons of heavy bombers (crows) would swoop low over the field, escorted by Combat Groups A, B, C and F. Groups A and F were composed of swallows, B of nightjars and C of blue jays. After this the troops would form column and, headed by the Mephitis Guards, make a circuit of the lawn and exit, center.

It was a lovely afternoon and the garden party was well attended. Three of Mrs. Pepperell's Colonel and General brothers were present, Peter's friend the Admiral was there, an Assistant Secretary of the Army and the Secretary for

Air. There were a couple of Cabinet Members and a great many others, all, of course, with wives and many daughters. Sam and two or three dusky assistants passed trays of refreshments. Barbara and Mrs. Pepperell went graciously from group to group commenting on the beauty of the weather and their guests' party frocks. Mr. Pepperell engaged in his usual argument with the General and wondered idly where Peter was.

Peter was behind the evergreens, busied with last minute details and carefully listening to the rising tide of chatter. When it had reached a deafening pitch he decided that X hour had arrived. Glancing at his wrist watch he started the phonograph, leaped into the saddle and took his place at the head of the Guards. At exactly X hour + 10 he raised his six-shooter and fired the starting signal.

The eager chipmunks sprang into their collars and, rattling and bouncing, the two tiny field guns dashed through the evergreens into the open, the gunners rigid as statues, arms folded on chests.

At the sound of the music, followed by the shot, the conversation had died away. Now the audience watched in openmouthed astonishment as the two guns executed thrilling two-wheeled turns and skidded into position. The gunners leaped down and unlimbered, the teams trotted the caissons briskly to the rear. The section commander raised one paw, dropped it, and the two salutes rang out, so perfectly timed that they seemed one explosion.

A dazed General slapped a Colonel on the shoulder. "By George," he exclaimed, "old A Battery never could equal that, never!"

Again Peter raised his six-shooter and fired a shot. He glanced around at the rigid ranks of his splendid Guards, swept his arm in a half circle and shouted "Forr-a-a-a-a-rd HARCH!"

As they emerged from the arching evergreens it was indeed a thrilling moment. Buck sidled and caracoled to the stirring music like a spirited Arabian. Behind him came the rhythmic tramp and the perfectly aligned ranks of the Mephitis Old Guards, their brilliantly striped tails, proudly arched, tossing like plumed shakos.

It was a thrilling moment for anyone who understood matters — unfortunately most of the guests did *not* understand. Sam took one look. His jaw dropped and his tray of glasses dropped — into the lap of the Admiral's wife. He stepped hastily backward, into the lily pool. The Assistant Secretary for War, a dainty sandwich halfway in his mouth, remained in a state of suspended animation. One of the Cabinet Members, tripping over a chair, joined Sam in the lily pool. Tables overturned, glasses crashed, trays scattered their lovely contents to be trampled by the fleeing throng.

Barbara, more quick-witted than most, sped over to Peter. "Oh, Peter darling," she cried. "Sound the retreat, do sound the retreat!"

Peter's eyes flashed. "The Old Guard NEVER retreats!"

he snapped. "By the right flank . . . HARCH!" Unperturbed by the general tumult the Guards continued their flawless drill.

Barbara and the Pepperells rushed about, reassuring the milling guests. The Admiral in his best quarterdeck voice roared commands and orders and gradually the panic was somewhat quieted. Most of the guests returned, although timidly. The Assistant Secretary finally finished his sandwich. At the completion of the drill there was even a scattering of applause. Sam, a dripping lily draped around his neck, sheepishly began to gather up trays and glasses.

Now Peter raised his right arm, dropped it, and again the field guns crashed out a simultaneous salute. It was the signal for the Aerial Review.

Almost at once could be heard the rush of a multitude of wings, a great sound of cawing, chirping and cackling, and a moment later the first Bomber Squadron swept in over the surrounding trees. Their formation was perfect, but it was unfortunate that their training period had been so short.

Their orders had been to swoop low over the field, but the squadron leader badly misjudged his distance and, followed obediently by the rest of the armada, swept entirely *too* low. Several party hats were dislodged from the heads of terrified ladies. Also, discipline among the fighter groups was lamentably bad. Many of the irresponsible young pilots took to dive bombing and stunting, especially the blue jays,

who indulged in an indiscriminate looting of the scattered cakes and sandwiches.

To make things worse the meadow mouse team of one of the supply wagons stampeded and despite the valiant efforts of the toad driver dashed madly among the quivering ankles of jittery guests. It was all too much for still shattered nerves; this time the panic was uncontrollable. Except for the Admiral, who stuck it out bravely, and the Cabinet Member, who was still in the house changing his wet clothes, the party was definitely over.

But through all the confusion the Mephitis Old Guards had stood rigidly at attention. Not a head had turned, not a whisker quivered. The gunners too, and the battery teams, had been models of statuelike steadfastness. Peter

was tremendously proud of them and told them so in a short speech before they were dismissed.

Later Mrs. Pepperell told Peter a few things too, in a somewhat longer speech. However, she was so pleased over the tray of glasses in the lap of the Admiral's wife (whom she disliked intensely) and the Cabinet Member in the lily pool (whom Mr. Pepperell disliked even more) that her talk was not at all a severe one. In fact she ended by praising the handsome appearance and exemplary conduct of the Mephitis Old Guards.

CHAPTER 4

Gus

When Peter was thirteen years old he had grown down
to a height of about four inches, which made him an ex-

tremely small boy. Mr. Pepperell, however, was not at all
upset, for he found him a wonderful help in the workshop.
Peter's tiny skillful hands could accomplish all sorts of
delicate operations that were quite impossible for normal-
sized fingers. When it came to rigging model ships he was
invaluable and he was able to walk about among the tracks
of the Pepperell Central Railroad making repairs and altera-
tions that formerly were most difficult.

It was about this time that he took up sailing, and it
was through sailing that he met Gus, a fortunate meeting
that was to have a great influence on his future, as well
as the future of the whole world.

One of Mr. Pepperell's larger models was a reproduction
of the America Cup defender *Resolute*. It was almost three
feet on the waterline, making it an ideal sailboat for Peter.
He trained a crew of field mice who soon became excep-
tionally smart and sure-footed sailors. There was a small
lake on the Pepperell property and here, when there was
any sort of a breeze, Peter and his crew had splendid sailing.

On this particular afternoon, a warm sunny June afternoon, the breeze had faded out completely, leaving the
Resolute becalmed in the middle of the pond. Most of the
crew were sleeping about the deck and Peter, at the wheel,
drowsed now and then. Gradually he became aware that a
large gray-backed sea gull had landed on the water and
was paddling gently over to the boat.

"Hi," Peter hailed.

"Howdy," the gull responded, "Wouldn't want a tow would you?"

"I don't think so, Peter said, "thanks just the same. We'll probably get a breeze pretty soon and it's sort of nice just sitting here."

"Sure is a swell day," the gull agreed. The field mice, who regarded the huge visitor with some misgiving, had unobtrusively gone below. "Tell 'em they needn't to worry," the gull laughed. "I ain't goin' to bother them none. Fish is *my* meat, as they say." His neck suddenly snapped out, there was a quick gulp, and the tail of a sizeable minnow slid down his throat. "Not much to these here fresh-water ones though."

"Do you live around here?" Peter asked.

"Nope. Baltimore," was the answer. "Down around the docks there is where I live mostly. Like to travel around though; see the world, as they say. That's a neat rig you got there."

"Yes," Peter agreed. "It's a scale model of the old *Resolute*. My father made it."

"Good job," the gull said approvingly. "My old man see the real one. Great old boat. Say," he asked suddenly, "you like to travel?"

"Well I don't know," Peter said, "I'd like to, but I've never traveled much. We usually go to Nantucket for a while in the summer, but that's about all. You see, I'm pretty small."

"Sure are," the gull chuckled, "but it's a real handy size at that. Good things come in small packages, as they say. Nantucket's a nice place, I've ben there. Ben most everywhere up and down the coast; Portland, Maine, Boston, Cape Cod, Gloucester (now there's a place, if you like fish), Long Island, New York, Philadelphia. Ben south too; Charleston, Brunswick, Savannah. Even ben to Florida, but I don't take much to that. Too hot, for one thing, and the sights you see on the beaches're just plain disgustin'. Know what I done down there? Dove after what I thought was one of them tropical fish and what do you suppose it was? A brazzeer, that's what. Pink too. Sick for a week. No sir, wouldn't live there if they give me the place, as they say."

"Have you ever been abroad?" Peter asked. "I'd like to go abroad."

"Well now, you know it's funny, your askin' that," the gull said, "because that's ben the one thing I've always wanted to do and never have. That's always ben my greatest ambition, as they say."

"Why don't you?" asked Peter. "You could fly over easily, couldn't you?"

"Sure, nothing to it. Trouble is I just don't care much about going alone. All right here along the coast where you know everybody pretty much. But them foreign parts, all them strange sights, and all them foreign gulls; there'd be nobody a fellow could talk to. Be lonesome, plain lonesome, that's what it'd be. What a fellow'd want would be somebody to go along with him. Congenial companionship, as they say.

"But these here birds around the docks down to Baltimore all's they want to do is sit there the rest of their lives, gettin' covered with soot and eating scraps off the ferry boats. No ambition, none of them. Ignorant too, ain't one of 'em would know the Tower of London from the Loover.

"Now me, I'm not much educated, but I do keep my eyes and ears open. All these here foreign ships comin' in to Baltimore, I hang around and listen to the sailors talking and the rats and even the ships' cats. I've picked up a lot, as they say. Do you know there's one cat there on one of them Eyetalian ships — he's seen the Spinks and the Pyramids! Yes sir! Seems he jumped ship at Alexandria and he hitchhiked his way out in the desert and he seen 'em — the Spinks *and* the Pyramids! Now ain't that something!"

"It certainly is," Peter agreed, "*I'd* like to see them. I'd like to see London Bridge too, that's always falling down, and Big Ben, and Blarney Castle and the Eiffel Tower and Bingen, fair Bingen on the Rhine. There's lots and lots of things I'd like to see."

At this moment the breeze suddenly came to life. The crew, their fear now gone, piled up from below, trimmed the sails and the *Resolute* got under way.

"Well, take it easy," the gull called, "I'll be seeing you again." His great wings flapped heavily a few times, he

skittered through the water and then, with wings outstretched he caught the rising breeze and soared gracefully away.

He came again the next day and for several days thereafter. It was hot June weather with few breezes, so each afternoon the gull would float bobbing beside the cockpit while he and Peter talked of strange seas and foreign places. Peter brought a lot of pictures from the National Geographic which the gull, whose name it now appeared was Gus, studied eagerly. "Well ain't that something!" he would say admiringly after looking at each one. "Ain't that something! I'm sure goin' to see *that* one of these days."

The third afternoon that he came there was no vestige of a breeze. Peter had sent the crew home and was sitting idly on the end of the dock. They had talked languidly of this and that when Gus abruptly asked, "Say, Pete, ever done any flying?"

"Why no," Peter admitted, "I never have."

"Well, how's about taking a ride? Perfectly safe. Lord, you don't weigh nothing. I've lugged two-three pounds of fish for miles an' miles and you don't weigh much more'n a sardine. You tell how you ride all over the country top of a rabbit and anybody that can ride a rabbit can certainly ride a gull. Ain't anything like as rough. Come ahead, step aboard."

Peter stepped carefully onto the solid gray back and settled himself just aft the wings. Gus's back was much broader than Buck's, but by working his legs well down into the feathers Peter was able to get a good knee grip.

"Now listen," Gus said, "takin' off's the only time is liable to be rough. You'll likely get splashed a bit and I've got to flap some to get off the water. But once we're off it and I can glide, it'll be as smooth as silk, as they say. Get holt of a couple of handfuls of feathers now and hang on tight. Here we go!"

Peter held on tightly, but the take-off was not nearly as rough as Buck's fence jumping. There was a spatter of spray, a few moments of vigorous flapping and then suddenly a miraculous quiet. Gus's great wings were spread wide, he soared and sailed in easy broad spirals, smoothly, quietly, ever upward.

It was the most thrilling moment Peter had ever known. Far below now he could see the lake, with the *Resolute* lying at her moorings. As they circled and soared he could see the house and all the grounds, he even saw Barbara and Mrs. Pepperell walking in the garden.

As they went higher and higher, mile after square mile spread out below them; brilliant checkerboard fields, dark patches of woodland, tiny houses, ribbon-like roads, the winding quicksilver of rivers. To the east they could see the white buildings of Washington, far to the west rose range after range of blue, shadow-spotted mountains.

"How're you doin', Pete?" Gus called.

"Oh, it's wonderful!" Peter gasped. "The most wonderful thing in all the world. It's *so* beautiful, and so still and smooth."

"Reckon it must be quite a kick if you've never ben up before," Gus chuckled. "Of course for me it's pretty old stuff, being practically raised on the wing, as they say. But I still like it. Where'd you care to go? Ever see the sights of Washington?"

"Only from the ground," Peter answered.

Gus swung into a long slanting glide and in a matter of moments they were circling over the spoke-like avenues and greenery of Washington. "Got a real plan to it," Gus said approvingly. "Only place I know of as has. New York now is just laid out like a griddle, sort of. Boston looks like something the cat got into, and the rest of them don't look like anything much. But this here's got a real plan to it, as they say."

They soared over the White House, around the beautiful Lincoln and Jefferson Memorials. They went up and down Pennsylvania Avenue. They skimmed over the Pentagon building and the new Art Gallery. As they approached the Washington Monument Gus suggested, "Let's take a breather, Pete; set and look around a minute. Grab holt now, because I'll have to stop sudden."

A few feet from the gleaming white pinnacle Gus's wings shot up in a vertical braking motion, then he settled down gently on the exact tip of the monument. They had only enjoyed the view a few moments when a guard thrust his head from the topmost window and shouted, "Hey, get off there. G'wan now, SHOO!"

Peter couldn't see him because of Gus's bulk, but he leaned out as far as he could and called indignantly, "We'll do nothing of the sort. I am a United States citizen and my father is a voter and a taxpayer. We have as much right here as anyone."

The guard dazedly withdrew his head. "A talking sea
gull," he half whispered in a shaky voice. "Cassidy, tonight
you go on the water wagon and there you stay."

Gus decided that they really should stop at the Capitol

before returning home. He lighted high up on the dome, just under the statue and walked slowly around the dome so that Peter could enjoy the whole panorama. Halfway around Peter suddenly gasped, "Gus, I feel awfully queer and dizzy. I think I'm going to faint."

"Groggy myself," Gus gulped. "Holt tight."

He took off and executed a series of wabbly spirals before the fresher air revived them both. "Well, of all the dumb clucks, I'm the prize one," Gus burst out. "Knew all about it and then go sit right amongst all them ventilators. Ought to have my head examined, as they say."

"But what about them?" Peter asked, still mystified.

"*About 'em!*" Gus snorted. "Gas, that's what. Hot air and gas. Why them ventilators come right out of the Senit Chamber."

They glided in to a gentle landing on the lake. Gus paddled past the moored *Resolute* and up to the dock. Peter stood a moment while they watched the lengthening shadows spread over the still water.

"Oh Gus," he burst out. "It was the most wonderful experience in my whole lifetime. I don't know how to thank you enough. Can we do it again, soon?"

"Soon as you want, is all right with me," Gus answered. "You know, there ain't nothing more lonesome than being way up there in the air all by yourself. It's swell — but lonesome. A little congenial companionship, as they say, makes it a lot more fun."

CHAPTER 5

Threat to Civilization

That evening Peter was eager to tell the family of his first
flight, but Mr. Pepperell did not seem in a receptive mood.
For two or three evenings now he had not gone near the
workshop, but had sat staring gloomily into the fireplace.

"Peter," Mrs. Pepperell finally said, "whatever's wrong
with you? You've sat around like a bear with a toothache
for three evenings now."

"I am worried," Mr. Pepperell said, "more worried than
I've ever been in my life." He got up and closed the hall
door, then drew his chair close to his wife and Barbara.

"I probably shouldn't mention this," he said in a low
voice, "but I'll go mad if I don't talk to someone. Remember, this is all strictly hush-hush, State secret of the highest

importance and all that. You must never breathe a word of it to anyone." Peter climbed up in Barbara's lap and all three listened attentively.

"Our department," Mr. Pepperell went on, "has recently learned, through channels which I cannot reveal, of the existence of a most frightful instrument of destruction."

"Atom bomb?" Barbara and Mrs. Pepperell both burst out.

"Infinitely worse. Compared to this the atomic bomb is a mere firecracker. The facts of the case are unbelievably peculiar. Our secret sources reveal that a certain scientist, whose name I must not mention, in a foreign country, which must remain unidentified, has developed this terrible explosive entirely on his own. He is a most erratic genius, many people believe him quite mad. He works in solitude, has no assistants and makes no notes; so this whole diabolical secret is hidden in this one warped brain.

"It has placed the government of his country in a strange quandary, for possession of this weapon would make them the most feared and powerful nation on earth. Yet they do not actually *possess* it. Moreover this scientist has threatened that, if interfered with in any way, he will merely drop the small capsule which contains his entire supply of this deadly substance. This would not only destroy him and his secret, but would wipe out his entire country, as well as most of Europe and a good part of Asia."

"Gee!" Peter murmured. Mrs. Pepperell and Barbara merely shuddered.

"Should his government by any chance manage to gain possession of this secret they could, no doubt, subjugate the entire world. On the other hand they are in hourly danger of complete extinction. They are, as the common expression has it, in a tough spot."

"Couldn't someone swipe it?" Peter asked, "while he was asleep or something?"

Mr. Pepperell smiled wryly. "He is probably the most elaborately guarded individual in the history of mankind. We are informed that he lives and works in an ancient castle, attended only by a few trusted old retainers. This castle is on an island in the center of a large lake, which I am not free to name. His government has circled every inch of the lake shore with heavily manned trenches, with tanks, flame throwers and machine guns, with antiaircraft batteries and every known form of radar and detection device. An umbrella of fighter planes patrols the skies day and night. His government is determined, naturally, that if they cannot have this secret, certainly no other country is going to have a chance at it. And of course they are determined that this madman shall not be disturbed lest, in a fit of irritation, he blow half a continent to bits."

"How do they know it's all that powerful?" Barbara asked. "Perhaps it's just a great hoax."

"Do you remember the great earthquake which rocked Europe and Asia last autumn?" Mr. Pepperell asked. "Well, it was not an earthquake at all. It was two grains of this substance, exploded in the exact center of the Gobi Desert. It was quite a convincing demonstration. As I remember, it dislodged several statues from the Cathedral of Notre Dame, stopped Big Ben, caused landslides in Switzerland and demolished a few miles of the Great Wall of China. No, I'm afraid it is no hoax, I only wish it were."

They all sat in stunned silence trying to take in the magnitude of this terrible threat. Finally Mrs. Pepperell gathered up her knitting and announced her intention of going to bed. "I just hope that horrible creature doesn't stub his toe or anything tonight," she said, "I really need a good sleep after this." Barbara also went up, leaving Peter and his father alone, both staring into the black fireplace.

"Father," Peter said thoughtfully. "Do you know, I think Gus and I could do something about this."

"About what — and who is Gus?" Mr. Pepperell asked absently.

Peter explained about his friendship with Gus and described the afternoon's flying experience. "I tried to tell you about it before," he said, "but you didn't pay much attention."

"Yes, yes," Mr. Pepperell agreed, "must have been lots of fun, very interesting I'm sure, quite a sensation. But what possible connection has all this with the subject we were discussing?"

"Well, just this," Peter said, "you say that scientist and

his castle are so carefully guarded. But what are they guarded *against*? They're just guarded against airplanes and men, soldiers and spies and that sort of thing; just the regular things they expect. They're not guarded against an ordinary seagull or a little boy the size of me. Why look, if that island is in a big lake there must be lots of gulls there. No one would ever pay any attention to Gus and no one would ever notice me. All Gus would have to do would be to land me on a window sill or on the roof and I'll bet I could go all over that old castle as much as I pleased. I'll bet I could swipe that little old capsule of stuff and bring it right back here just as easy as not."

The reason that Mr. Pepperell was one of the highest figures in the State Department was that he had an imagination and an open mind. He almost never said "Tut, tut," or "Nonsense, nonsense," or "Quite impossible, quite impossible," when a new or unusual idea was proposed. Now he sucked on his pipe for a long time before answering.

"Son," he finally said, "your plan seems so simple and practical that there must be something wrong with it. But think as I can, I see no reason why it might not work. The chief difficulty will be in persuading the Department to consider it seriously. It has three great disadvantages; first it is simple, second, it is practical, and third it won't cost a cent. If it called for an appropriation of a few million or, better still, a billion or so, it would be easy. As it is, I shall have to work hard. However I will attack the Secretary himself tomorrow. He is a man of real vision, if I can convince him all may be well. It might work — yes by George — it might work."

"Gus has always wanted to go abroad," Peter said, "this would be a great chance. I'm sure he would co-operate. May I tell him all about it?"

"I think he can be trusted," Mr. Pepperell smiled. "Now let's go to bed." He left Peter in his room and as he went down the hall Peter could hear him still murmuring, "*It might work*, yes, it might just be the answer!"

The next afternoon Peter could hardly wait for Gus's arrival. When he did come Peter poured out the whole tale of the mad scientist and of his own plan for frustrating him. Gus listened attentively, occasionally exclaiming, "Well now, ain't that something."

"Man, oh man," he shouted as Peter finished, "looks like we're goin' to get that trip to Europe sooner'n we figured on. No reason why we can't pull this off, none at all. First thing, though, we got to convince these here Washington bigwigs. Now who's this here Secatary you spoke about?"

"The Secretary of State," Peter explained. "He's head of the whole State Department."

"Your old man's boss, hey? Know where his office is at?"

"Yes," Peter answered, "It's a big one on the southeast corner of the State Department Building, fourth floor.

Father's is on the same floor, but on the southwest corner."

"Good," Gus said. "Let's us do some convincin' right now. Come on, hop aboard."

As they soared rapidly toward Washington Gus revealed what he had in mind. "Now look," he said, "here's what I figgered we'd do. We just sail around quiet like and look things over. We find a office that's sort of empty lookin'; it's hot and all the windows will likely be open. I light on the window sill, you hop off and go in. Then it's up to you. With your handy little size you'd ought to be able to sneak around most anywheres you please. You'll swipe some little thing, maybe out of this Secatary's office. Then you come out on the window sill, wave your handkerchief and I swoop down and pick you up. That ought to prove to 'em how easy it'd be for a couple of smart fellers like us to pull off this little capsull swiping job over there in Europe."

It seemed an excellent plan and it worked out even more perfectly than they had dared hope. Soaring slowly past his father's window Peter saw the Secretary himself, standing in earnest conversation with Mr. Pepperell.

"He's in father's office, the Secretary is," Peter said excitedly. "Hurry up Gus, his office is probably empty."

A swoop past the window revealed that the Secretary's office *was* vacant, moreover that his desk stood close beside the window — and the window was open. "Duck soup," Gus chuckled and landed lightly on the sill. Peter hopped off, grasped the heavy curtain and swung over to the Secretary's desk.

"O.K." Gus called softly, "wave your handkerchief when you want me. I'll just cruise around."

One upper drawer of the desk was open, so Peter dropped in. He landed on a small box which, he was overjoyed to discover, contained a number of capsules. On the cover was written *One after each meal, Dr. Pulsifer*. Peter extracted one capsule, then giggling slightly, dumped the box containing the rest into the wastebasket. At this moment he heard a rattling of the doorknob and had just time to duck down behind the desk clock when the Secretary of State entered.

The Secretary, looking very handsome but very worried, sat down at his desk and hiccupped slightly. His hand went to the drawer and rummaged around for a moment. Then he snatched the drawer open and searched it thoroughly.

"Miss Putty," he shouted irritably, "who's been messing in my desk? Where is my medicine?"

As Miss Putty rushed in and fluttered about, Peter stepped from behind the clock, holding the capsule.

"Here, Mr. Secretary," he said quietly, "is the mysteriously missing capsule."

"Good Lord," the Secretary stuttered. "you aren't — you must be Pepperell's young boy — "

"Exactly," Peter said. "Peter Peabody Pepperell III. It's quite a long name for anyone my size. I had the honor of meeting you at home — when I was larger. Now what I

wanted to prove to you sir," he went on as the Secretary slowly lowered himself into his chair, "was just this. Suppose that you were a certain foreign scientist, whose name can't be mentioned, and that this capsule contained a certain deadly secret. Do you see how easily it could be swiped?"

He tucked the capsule under his arm, swung to the window sill and waved his handkerchief. Almost at once Gus lighted beside him.

"Sir, you will find the rest of your medicine in the waste-basket," Peter called as he mounted. He waved pleasantly to the Secretary who still sat, openmouthed, in his chair and Gus dove off in a long soaring glide.

They returned home in high glee and sat for an hour or two on the dock, eagerly discussing plans for the European trip, which they now felt was assured. "If that deemonstration didn't convince that there Mr. Secatary," Gus chortled, "nothin' will."

The sun was low and Gus was about to take off for Baltimore when Mr. Pepperell came rushing down the path to the lake.

"Great news, Peter," he called excitedly before he even reached them. "Your trip is on. The Chief has suddenly decided that your plan is entirely feasible. I worked on him all morning, but didn't seem to be getting anywhere. Then after lunch he rushed in and said he was convinced it would work. Don't know what got into him, but he's all for it now. I'm taking a two weeks' leave to make preparations."

Peter slapped Gus on the back and Gus gave out a long *Graw-w-w-a-k* of pleasure. "Father," Peter said, "I'd like you to meet my friend Gus. He's really made all this possible."

"It is a pleasure and a great honor," Mr. Pepperell said solemnly.

"Pleased to meetcha, as they say," Gus responded. "Be seein' you tomorrow."

Total Mobilization

Next morning Mr. Pepperell plunged eagerly into his preparations. His first project was the building of a small car, to be strapped to Gus's back. It would give Peter shelter from bad weather, a place to sleep, to carry extra clothes, food and water. Mr. Pepperell took careful measurements of Gus and retired to his workshop, from which he scarcely emerged for a week.

When informed of Peter's plan Mrs. Pepperell and Barbara had both been quite upset at the thought of the risks involved. However, Mrs. Pepperell's long training as a member of an Army family now stood her in good stead. Although she may have spent many unhappy hours when alone, in the presence of others she wore an air of cheery optimism.

She and Barbara busied themselves making a flying suit for Peter. For this Barbara sacrificed a long evening glove of the softest kid, which, when lined with moleskin, promised to make a warm and practical material. The cutting and stitching required much patient labor, but the result amply justified their efforts. Peter was delighted with it and Gus was loud in praise.

While the others were thus occupied, Peter and Gus spent most of their time down on the dock looking at pictures of foreign places and buildings. As they had not yet been told the name of the country to which they were going it was not possible to plan an exact itinerary. However Peter did make a long list of the things they most wanted to see if time allowed.

"It sure is somethin' to be eddicated," Gus said admiringly. "Now me, I got no eddication to speak of and I wouldn't have known nothin' about most of these here places, or where they was even. If I'd a gone over there by myself or with some of these iggorant fellers from Baltimore I'd a just blundered around and likely missed most of the best sights. Sure am lucky to have a eddicated pal like you along, Pete."

Peter had many other things to attend to, too. The *Resolute* was laid up and her crew dismissed. Buck was made General of the Army. He had been somewhat hurt over Peter's interest in flying, which had pretty well ended their rides together, but this appointment soothed his hurt feelings entirely.

Then there were a great many visits from young men of the State Department, who asked Peter endless questions and filled out endless forms. "Look," Peter said, "I'm not supposed to take all those papers along, am I? Why Gus would never be able to take off with that load of junk, let alone get anywhere."

"Oh, no indeed," the young man assured him. "All your maps, instructions, credentials and so forth will be reduced on microfilm and rolled in aluminum tubes. They will be smaller than half a match stick and of course much lighter."

With all these goings-on a week passed quickly, till one afternoon Mr. Pepperell emerged from the workshop with the car. It was the most carefully planned and beautifully executed model he had ever built.

To reduce wind resistance it was shaped rather like half a pear. It was made mostly of magnesium and therefore weighed almost nothing. The main part forward contained a bunk for Peter, under which were lockers for his clothes. Just aft of this was a compartment for food and back of that a small water tank. The main cabin which held the bunk was covered by a dome of clear Plexiglas and fastened to the extreme front was a small armchair. The bottom of the car was shaped to exactly fit the curves of Gus's back and there were two light but strong straps to hold it firmly in place. These were fitted with safety buckles that could be unfastened in a second in case of an emergency. Just aft the food compartment was a tiny flagstaff.

Peter was wild with delight and Gus was so overwhelmed with admiration that he could only repeat, "Well now, ain't that something, *Ain't* that something." Mr. Pepperell proudly opened all the lockers and explained some of the finer points.

"You will notice that I have made no provision for heating the car. I have, however, left the bottom open, under the main cabin. Fitting tightly as it does to Gus's back the heat of his body should warm the car sufficiently. Also of course in the daytime the sun on the Plexiglas dome will furnish a great deal of heat.

"Your water tank can be easily replenished. This series of grooves in the top of the car all run down to an opening in the tank. Simply remove the plug and the slightest

shower or even a heavy dew will fill it quickly."

"Well now, ain't *that* somethin'," Gus admired.

"I have filled the water tank," Mr. Pepperell went on, "and placed in the car an amount of ballast equal to what your clothes, food, blankets and so on will weigh. Even then I do not think it is very heavy."

Gus picked up the car by one of the straps and hefted it with a practiced air. "Don't weigh scarcely nothin'," he pronounced. "Why Lord, I've carried five times the weight of that in my stummick, in the way of fish, 'thout any trouble. If necessary I could eat light and often, but even that won't be necessary. Why'nt we give 'er a try?"

"I thought a trial flight would be a good idea," Mr. Pepperell agreed. He and Peter quickly strapped on the car and at that moment Mrs. Pepperell and Barbara appeared. Barbara bore a tiny American flag, while Mrs. Pepperell carried a small vial of amber-colored fluid. As Barbara attached the flag to the staff Mrs. Pepperell announced, "This craft must be christened and christened correctly. What is its name, by the way?"

No one had thought about a name, so there was quite a discussion. Peter wanted it called either *Gus* or *Joe DiMaggio*, while Mr. Pepperell held out for something more dignified such as *The 17 Freedoms* or *The Spirit of Tolerance*. Finally Gus was appealed to.

"Well, I wouldn't know," he said, "but seein' as Pete here figgered out the whole scheme, I'd sorta think it oughta be called *Pete's Ideer*."

"Perfect," Mrs. Pepperell cried. Her voice caught a bit, but she bravely pronounced, "I hereby christen you *Pete's Ideer*," and smashed the tiny vial of champagne on the prow of the car.

Peter hopped aboard and settled himself in the seat. "All right, Gus," he called, "let's go."

Gus took off from the dock on a long slant, caught a breeze and rose up and up in swift ascending circles. "How you doin', Pete?" he called. "You and the car still there? Wouldn't know it by the weight. Ain't nothin' at all, as they say."

He banked and circled and dove, sometimes skimming the surface of the lake. He shot over treetops, landed on the water and took off again in a cloud of spray. He executed every maneuver he could think of while Peter, seated snugly in the chair, whooped exultantly. Finally, Gus swooped in to a spectacular landing on the dock where the eager family waited.

"Couldn't be better," he pronounced as Mr. Pepperell unstrapped the car. "No weight, no hindrance to flyin', nothin' wrong. Pete, I don't mind telling you your old man's an A number one mechanic. Why he wants to waste his time in that there State Department is beyont me. He could get a real job in the B & O shops any time."

For the next few days the car, now neatly lettered PETE'S IDEER, stood on the living room table while Barbara and Mrs. Pepperell packed it. Tiny sheets, pillows and blankets were placed on the bunk. The clothes lockers were filled with clean shirts, underwear and pajamas. Peter's evening clothes were included, for he would have to visit many of the Embassies, and the State Department was most particular about such things. Mr. Pepperell had even included a locker for towels, soap, toothpaste and a toothbrush.

The food compartment was packed tight with minute cans containing every sort of food, including chewing gum,

salted peanuts, chocolate bars and a large "Thermos" bottle for hot cocoa.

As the small aluminum containers filled with microfilmed documents arrived from the State Department they were fastened by clamps to the wall of the cabin. At almost the last moment Barbara thought of a parachute, but Peter only laughed. "Why goodness," he said. "Gus often drops a fish, just for fun, and catches it again before it's dropped twenty feet. If I fell off he'd have me by the seat of the britches before I'd hardly started."

Everything now being prepared, the start was set for noon of June 21st. On the evening of the 20th, Mr. Pepperell called Peter into the workshop for final instructions.

"Son," he said, "of course you still do not know where you are going, and I cannot tell you. It has been decided that it

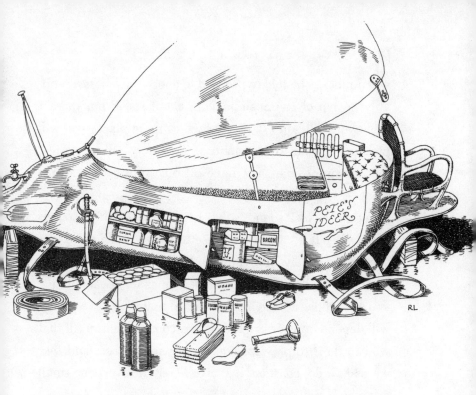

would be much safer if you do not receive final information until reaching Europe. There might be a leak somewhere. Therefore you will proceed first to the American Embassy in London. A map of London in tube #1 shows the exact location. There will be a large American flag spread on the roof and they will be expecting you."

"Oh, London. That's grand," Peter interrupted. "Gus has always wanted to see the Tower of London and I want to see them changing the Guard at Buckingham Palace and Big Ben and lots of things."

"In London," Mr. Pepperell went on, "you will receive some instruction and certain information. From there you will doubtless be told to proceed to another Embassy, probably in one of the Scandinavian countries. From there I think you will go to Paris. At each of these places you will pick up additional instructions. This may all seem silly, but we simply dare not have all our information in one place."

"I don't think it sounds silly," Peter said, "I think it sounds wonderful. It'll give us a chance to see so much more."

"On the really vital point," Mr. Pepperell continued, "that of actually securing this deadly menace, I cannot give you any advice at all. Once arrived at that castle everything will depend on your brightness and common sense. All that we can do is to pray for your safety and success and that we will all do, constantly. I have here, however, one small gift which may prove useful."

He presented Peter with a tiny sword in a beautiful gold scabbard. It was not much larger than a large pin and was hung from a stout leather belt.

"This is not exactly an ordinary sword," Mr. Pepperell explained. "It is really a small hypodermic needle, filled with the most powerful drug known to modern science. An infinitesimal amount of this drug will render anyone unconscious for at least twelve hours. I hope you will not need to use it, but if you ever should, jab it in firmly and give the hilt a slight squeeze. The effect is instantaneous."

Peter thanked him and together they fastened the sword to a clip in the cabin of *Pete's Ideer*. Then they went to bed.

CHAPTER 7

Wings over Manhattan

The departure next day was made with little ceremony. The State Department, being still afraid of a leak, wanted everything kept as quiet as possible. So there were only a few people there; the Pepperells, of course, and Barbara, their friend the Admiral and two of Peter's Colonel uncles. Then there were the Secretary of State, the Assistant Secretaries of War, Navy and Air Force, each with a young man to carry his briefcase. The head of the F.B.I. was there, a Senator and a Major of Marines who had invited himself. Their chauffeurs, six Secret Service men, Sam the butler and the rest of the household servants formed a background audience.

Peter looked extremely handsome in his new flying suit. He didn't really need it, for it was a rather hot day, but he wore it to please Barbara and his mother.

Everyone shook hands with everyone else, except the Major, and all admired the conveniences of the car, now completely loaded and strapped to Gus's back. Gus himself was bored with the delay and eager to be off.

"Whyn't we get goin'?" he grumbled to Peter. "What's the sense to all this here flumdummery? I ben promisin' myself a meal of them Hudson River shads fer the past week and I'd jest as soon get at it."

Peter hastened the Secretary's speech by kissing all his family and climbing up to his seat at the front of the car. As he did so there was a familiar rattling sound and he was delighted to see Buck and the army deploying in handsome order on a small lawn by the water's edge. The Mephitis Old Guards marched with their usual faultless precision, the two field guns dashed smartly into position and prepared to fire. As the Secretary finished his speech Peter raised his hand and the guns barked out their salute.

"All right, Gus," Peter said. "Let's go."

Without further ceremony Gus took off and made one swiftly rising circuit of the lake. They passed over the dock and its group of upturned faces and waving handkerchiefs. They saw two tiny puffs of white smoke and heard two faint bangs as the guns fired a final salute. A moment later the dock and the lake and the house had all vanished in the distance.

Gus took a northeasterly course. "Thought we might's well go up the coast," he explained. "Decent air and avoids all them factories. No use gettin' ourselfs all sooted up if we don't have to."

They soared over the beautiful green farms of Maryland and Delaware, over the glittering waters of Chesapeake Bay and Delaware Bay, crossed the southern tip of New Jersey and were soon sailing northward along the Jersey coast. Gus flew low, just skimming the tops of the breakers, while Peter amused himself looking through his field glasses at the crowded beaches, the great hotels and the colorful boardwalks.

In what seemed an incredibly short time they swept in over Sandy Hook, crossed the Lower Bay and were circling the Statue of Liberty. "Let's take a breather, Pete," Gus suggested as he lighted gently on the extreme top of Miss Liberty's head, "while we look around and sort of co-ordinate our plans, as they say."

Most of New York and the Jersey shore were dimmed

by a bank of smoky haze, but the great skyscrapers rose grandly above it, their tops shining fairylike in the warm sun.

"You wanted some shad, didn't you Gus?" Peter asked.

"Countin' on it, countin' on it considerable," Gus answered. "How'd you care to take in a ball game, whilst I do a bit of fishin'?"

"Oh grand," Peter exclaimed. "The Yankees are playing the Red Sox today and maybe Joe DiMaggio will knock a homer."

"Likely two," Gus chuckled. "O.K. Yankee Stadium the next stop."

Gus knew the location of the stadium well and a few minutes later they landed on the roof of the grandstand, directly back of home plate. Peter removed his flying suit, which was uncomfortably warm, packed it neatly in the clothes compartment, got out his field glasses and settled himself snugly at the foot of a flagstaff.

"Ain't you forgot somethin'?" Gus laughed. "Always heard's how a ball game ain't nothing without peanuts."

"That's right, I *had* forgotten," Peter said, and unpacked a can of salted peanuts from the food locker. As he settled himself again Gus called, "O.K. Pete. Enjoy yourself. And don't worry. I'll take a look now and then and I'll be back at the end of the ninth. Right on the dot, as they say."

Peter was already enjoying himself. It was a perfect day and a well-nigh perfect game. The sun was hot, the air was

still and the game was nip and tuck all the way. Through his powerful field glasses Peter had a wonderful view of everything that went on. There was one uncomfortable moment when a high foul just grazed the flagstaff beside which he was sitting, otherwise it was pure bliss. Joe DiMaggio did hit two home runs; the second, in the ninth inning with two men on base, broke up the ball game.

Just as the tremendous roar rose from the stands and people started spilling out over the field, Gus arrived. Peter was too excited to notice that his friend seemed quite swollen in body and slow in movement. He scrambled up into the seat and cried, "Oh Gus, do you suppose we could speak to him?"

"Sure," Gus said, "why not?"

He took off and made a heavy dive toward home plate, where a milling crowd of players were congratulating the hero. Gus swept within a few feet of their astonished faces while Peter, leaning out, screeched ecstatically, "Great work Joe. You were wonderful!"

"*Did you see what I seen?*" one goggle-eyed player asked another.

"I saw a sea gull, or I see a saw gull — I don't know what I seen," was the dazed answer. "Somethin' I et, likely."

DiMaggio rubbed a hand over his eyes and shook his head. "Looking into the sun too much," he muttered. "Got to see the Doc about some new sunglasses."

They all turned to watch the heavily laboring gull as he flapped frantically to gain altitude. "Jest some new kind of an advertisement stunt, I guess," one of the players said. "Got a little radio or something tied on him. Prob'ly was supposed to say something about paper towels or razor blades. He ain't making out very good."

Gus was indeed having trouble in making out of the stadium. It took a great deal of flapping to clear the bleachers and they made it by just a few feet. He banked sharply and glided down to the Harlem River.

"Phew!" he grunted, as they skimmed along the river, shooting under bridges and dodging puffing tugboats. "That certainly was a tough one. Pete, don't you never leave me loose again when there's shads around. Overindulged, that's what I done. Overindulged and then some, as they say. I'm chock full of shads clean to the ears. Should have knowed better at my age, but I've got a sort of a weakness that way."

"Do you feel all right now?" Peter asked anxiously as they swept along the East River and out over the Sound.

"Feeling fine, never better," Gus chuckled. "Just a bit overloaded is all. Be all right presently."

They sailed along down the Sound, Long Island on their right, the haze-shrouded shore of Connecticut on their left. Soon they passed Montauk Light on the tip of Long Island and headed out over the clear blue waters of the Atlantic.

"Figgered we'd best spend the night to Nantucket," Gus said. "Nice quiet place. Ought to have a good night's sleep before we really shove off. May have to do a lot of night flying, all depends on the weather."

"Oh Nantucket, that's grand," Peter exclaimed. "We go there every summer. The water's so nice and there's wonderful fish — "

Gus burped so violently that the car shook. "If you'd just as soon, Pete," he reproved, "please let's not mention fish for a while. Them shads!"

Behind them the sun was nearing the horizon, the blue of the ocean became steadily deeper. Now far ahead they could see the white beaches of Nantucket floating on the water like shavings from a giant's plane. They swept in over the moors where the little bays and ponds shone like bits

of sky-blue mirrors set in a rich tapestry. Over the old gray town they went, past the glittering golden dome of the meetinghouse and on up harbor.

"Figgered Polpis harbor'd be our best spot," Gus said as he banked and settled gently on the still surface of the little bay. The sun was just setting now, the water was like burnished gold, etched with the sharp black of tall cattails. The rolling moors were a misty purple spotted with deep blue shadows. Gus paddled gently up a tiny inlet where the water was even more still. Somewhere in the reeds a duck quawked sleepily.

"Well, I reckon this ought to do," Gus yawned. "Better get yourself some supper, Pete, and a good long sleep. No supper for me though. Them shads was breakfast, lunch, dinner, tea *and* supper, far as I'm concerned."

"I have some bicarbonate of soda," Peter suggested. "Would you care for a dose?"

"Nope, thanks. Sleep's all I crave." Gus stretched his neck, ruffled his feathers. "G'night Pete," he mumbled sleepily. "See you in the morning." He tucked his head under his wing and in a moment was snoring steadily.

Peter supped on two Smithfield ham sandwiches, a slice of cake and a cup of hot cocoa. He washed his face and hands, brushed his teeth, undressed and donned his pajamas. Then he said his prayers and climbed into bed.

It was dark now; through the Plexiglas dome the whole sky winked with millions of stars. Along the far beach one or two picnic fires flickered long red reflections across the dark water. Far to the north Great Point lighthouse shone steadily. To the south, just above the moor hills, Sankaty Light flashed its alternating beam.

The cabin rocked ever so gently. Peter slept.

CHAPTER 8

The Long Hop

Peter waked just before sunrise. The little cabin was flooded
with clear light. For a moment he couldn't remember where
he was, then he leaped out of bed, opened the dome and
hopped out on Gus's broad back. At the moment Gus was
in the act of swallowing a small minnow.

"Good morning Gus," Peter called happily. "I see you've
got your appetite back."

"Just a couple of little minners is all." Gus grinned sheepishly and changed the subject. "Say, ain't this a swell morning? Great day fer the races, as they say."

It was a gorgeous morning. A fresh breeze sent little ripples splashing and chuckling along the shore. The sun, now just peeping above the ocean, shone warmly on the high sand cliffs and white beaches. Outside the harbor busy little fishing boats butted through the brisk sea kicking up bursts of spray.

With a whoop Peter tossed off his pajamas and dove in. He splashed and cavorted, swam around Gus two or three times and then made for a small sandy beach. Here he raced back and forth in the sunshine until he was thoroughly dry and warm.

Gus waddled up on the beach and settled in the warm sand. "If you wouldn't mind taking off this contraption fer a while, Pete," he suggested, "I might do a bit of ablutin' myself."

Peter unstrapped the car, dressed quickly and set about getting breakfast, for which he was now more than ready. There was orange juice, some cold biscuits, bacon and still plenty of hot cocoa. While Gus splashed and dove, and snapped up a few more minnows, Peter built a small fire, broiled his bacon and warmed up the biscuits. Never had a breakfast tasted better, even Gus consented to accept a few biscuits.

Peter washed up the dishes, repacked the food locker and made his bed neatly. He inspected the water tank which was still almost full and announced everything ready. Gus, who had been sunning and preening his feathers, yawned, stretched and then squatted down so that Peter could replace the car. This done and the straps snugly fastened there seemed no reason for further delay.

"Now Pete," Gus said, "this here is the long hop, but there ain't nothin' to get worried about. *We* can always set down on the water and take a breather whenever we feel like it, unlike them dumb aireoplanes. I figger it ought to take about two days and nights, maybe more, maybe less. All depends on the weather."

"They gave me a lot of maps and charts and tables," Peter said. "Ocean currents, wind currents, prevailing drifts — all sorts of things."

"Oh them," Gus snorted. "Look Pete. I ain't eddicated enough to understand them things anyhow, but I always figger if you're going somewhere, why just go there. Straight line's the shortest distance between two points, as they say. We're goin' to London ain't we, so let's just go to London — and fergit them blasted charts."

"That's fine with me," Peter laughed. "I probably couldn't understand them either. Let's go."

Gus took a short run down the beach, spread his wings to the fresh breeze and they were off. They soared over the outer bar, shot past Great Point Light and in a moment were winging over the broad Atlantic.

Gus was really flying now and it was clear why he

despised man-made aids. His skill and instincts were a thousand times more sure than any clumsy wind chart. Sometimes he flew high, sometimes just skimmed the surface of the water, always riding the most favoring breeze. There were long slanting glides at terrific speeds, breathtaking ascents, slow circlings and then a new series of dives. Peter had no way of judging their exact speed, but he could see that when they overtook ships going their way they passed them as though they were at anchor. Once they fell in with a Europe bound plane and for miles Gus raced it, easily keeping alongside.

Gus talked little while flying, his mind was on his work, but Peter had a wonderful time watching ships through his field glasses. They were following the main shipping lane, so there was scarcely a time when there wasn't a ship somewhere in sight. There were stubby freighters, wallowing and kicking up huge wakes, slow heavy tankers, now and then a liner. They saw the graceful white winged Gloucester fishing schooners making for the Banks, and the slowly circling trawlers. Once or twice there were naval vessels; two knife-sharp destroyers, a long sleek-lined cruiser, once a dark, venomous-looking submarine.

Peter was so absorbed that he failed to notice it was far past lunch time when Gus suddenly spoke. "There she is," he called, "that's what I was lookin' fer." He went into a long racing glide.

Looking ahead Peter saw the most beautiful ship they

had yet met. Even at this height she looked large, yet she slid through the water with far less fuss and effort than vessels one third her size. Her scrubbed decks gleamed white, her lifeboats and upper works shone with brilliant paint.

"The *Queen Mary*," Gus exclaimed jubilantly, " — and my lunch. They feed good, they do. Best there is. Better make hay while the sun shines, as they say. Prob'ly be my last decent meal fer some time."

They circled the great ship two or three times. Peter could see the blue-clad officers on the bridge, gaily dressed

passengers strolling the decks, games in progress, children playing.

Gus settled gently in the creamy wake and almost at once speared a piece of French pastry. "Lavish, that's what it is," he chortled when the pastry had been swallowed, "Plain lavish." He snapped up a few stalks of celery, a sardine on toast and an untouched slice of honeydew melon. "Horse doovers and all," he said jubilantly. "In near shore you'd have to fight for a treat like this, but out here a feller can dine like a gentleman, as they say."

Peter, reminded that it was long past his own lunch time, brought out some deviled eggs, a couple of chicken sandwiches and a slab of chocolate cake. He lunched pleasantly, while Gus continued his happy foraging.

"Don't overindulge now, Gus," Peter laughed.

"Needn't to worry," Gus chuckled contentedly. "Shads is my only weakness. This here's real dainty fodder."

He took off easily and they were again on their way.

The long morning, the dazzle of the sea and the lulling motion of their progress all combined to make Peter dreadfully sleepy. Toward midafternoon he announced his intention of taking a nap.

"Good ideer, Pete," Gus agreed. "Go to it. May grab a bit of shut-eye myself, often do on long trips. Only trouble nowadays is these blasted aireoplanes. Close your eyes a few minutes and one of 'em's liable to slice you in half. Think they owned the sky. We're off their route now though, so it's all right."

Peter stretched out on the bunk and almost immediately fell into a delicious sleep. When he woke the level rays of the setting sun shone in the cabin. From the bobbing motion he judged they were on the water. He stretched and went out on Gus's back.

"Well," Gus greeted him, "hope you had a good nap. Slep' some myself. Just seen a freighter goin' by and decided it was time for supper. Nothin' fancy like the *Queen Mary*, but sustaining, very sustaining."

Peter got out some food and ate a light supper while they watched the sun sink in a glorious bed of golden clouds.

"Real purty," Gus commented, "but personally I don't care for the looks of it. Figger we'll keep on flying tonight. Had real good weather so far and we might's well ride our luck while we got it, as they say. Sort of like night flying myself, quiet-like and you can sleep half the time. Go to bed when you feel like, Pete; see you in the mornin'." He flapped a few times and they soared on eastward.

Peter sat in the chair for a while, while the stars appeared one by one until the dome of the sky was a brilliant twinkling canopy. Once in a while they passed the lights of a ship and could see its faintly luminous wake. Gus sailed in long, gentle, sleepy swoops. Finally Peter bid him good night and stumbled in to bed.

Later, he did not know how much later, Peter was waked by violent tossings of the car and a roaring, swishing sound. He hastily switched on his flashlight, but could see

nothing through the roof but rushing water. He shut off the flashlight and clung to the handholds on the cabin wall. As his eyes grew more accustomed to the darkness he could occasionally see the dim blur of Gus's streaming wings flapping and banking at wild angles. A flash of lightning gave a clearer view and made it plain that they were caught in a heavy storm. Peter dared not open anything, there was no way of communicating with Gus, so he just held tight.

There was a dive so sharp that he almost lost his grip and an even louder roaring. He caught a fleeting glimpse of a huge plane battling its way through the gale, its lights dim and sheets of rain streaming from the wings.

Peter *was* frightened, there was no denying that, but he had complete confidence in Gus and gradually relaxed. He was delighted to find that the car had not leaked a drop, everything was tight and shipshape. He opened the cap of the water tank which filled up immediately.

Then, as suddenly as a train coming out of a tunnel, they came out of the storm. The slashing roar of the rain ceased. The wild dives changed to the usual soothing glides. The Plexiglas dome dried off and a canopy of brilliant stars appeared. Peter stepped out on Gus's sodden back and hailed him.

"Hi, Pete, how you doin'?" Gus called. "Quite a shower. Sorry I couldn't miss it, but I sort of got caught nappin', as they say. Wouldn't a liked to a ben in that plane we passed. How'd the car make out?"

"Fine," Peter answered. "Didn't leak a drop. Don't you want to take a rest? It must have been tough for you."

"Reckon I will," Gus agreed. "Calm as a millpond here. No use rushin' things." He glided down to a quiet landing.

The water was mirror smooth with only a gentle almost imperceptible swell. Gus ruffled his feathers, yawned a sleepy good night, tucked his head under his wing and at once began to snore. Peter climbed into bed and pulled up the blankets. They rose and fell gently on the soft swell, the stars glittered brilliantly. In a moment Peter also was asleep.

The next day was very like the first. The sun was brilliant, the winds favoring. They made splendid progress.

About midmorning Peter was thrilled by the sight of an old bark under full sail. Gus swooped down and circled around it several times so that Peter could view it from every angle. It was a lovely sight.

Shortly after lunch they noticed a great many more vessels than they had seen before. There were rusty little freighters belching great clouds of black smoke, small coastwise ships, trawlers and fishing smacks by the dozen.

"Do you know what, Pete?" Gus said suddenly. "We're way ahead of schedule. That storm must have give us a big boost. We're gettin' clost to England, that's what. Ought to sight land any time now."

Peter eagerly trained his field glasses on the horizon ahead and some time later shouted excitedly, "There it is Gus. Land ho! Dead over your beak."

"Seen it a while ago," Gus chuckled, "and what's more I know what it is. It's Land's End, that's what, and over there to the right is the Lizard. Hit 'er plumb on the nose, we did. Not bad navigatin' for a iggorant feller from Baltimore, hey?"

As they swept past the Lizard Peter consulted his map of England. "You're right Gus, of course. That must be Eddystone Light ahead and over to the left there is Plymouth where the Pilgrims set sail."

"So that's where they brung the Rock from," Gus commented. "Right purty little place. Don't see why they wanted to leave it fer any dreary old sand spit like Cape Cod."

They soared along the South Coast, crossed the Isle of Wight, its waters dotted with hundreds of little sailboats and swung inland, north toward London.

"Croydon Airport is just south of London, maybe we'd better avoid that," Peter suggested.

"*I'll* say," Gus grunted. "Blasted planes'll be thicker'n fleas on a dog's back. That there map of yours is some use after all." He swung sharply to the left and they soon crossed a small winding river.

"Hold on Gus," Peter called, "that must be the Thames. We can follow it right down into London."

"*That?*" Gus snorted. "Why that ain't nothin' more'n a fair-sized crick." Nevertheless he banked and followed the course of the winding stream. "Must be it," he admitted a

moment later. "Sure is disappointing. Always thought the Thames was a river. That cloud of smoke ahead is likely London. What's this here place we're passing now?"

"Windsor Castle," Peter announced, consulting the map again, "where the Royal Family lives part of the time."

"Well now, ain't that somethin'," Gus said. "Sure pays to be eddicated. I'd never have known what it was, might have missed it entirely. Not that it would have mattered a whole lot," he added.

As they neared the city Peter got out his large-scale map of London and Gus soared high up above the smoke cloud until the city was spread out below them exactly like the map. In this way it was easy to locate the Embassy; they could even see dimly the American flag spread out on the roof. Gus circled down and a moment later they landed before the astonished gaze of two of the Embassy's young men. One of them was dusting the continually falling soot from the flag, while the other had obviously been scanning the sky through a pair of field glasses.

"Er — ah — Master Pepperell, I presume?" the young man with the field glasses asked as Peter somewhat stiffly

descended from Gus's back. "The Ambassador is having tea. I shall fetch him directly." Almost at once the Ambassador burst out onto the roof, teacup still in hand.

"Well, well, well, so you made it?" he exclaimed.

" 'Course we made it," Gus muttered to Peter. "Wouldn't be here if we hadn't. Say Pete," he went on, "I'm not much on this Embassy stuff. I want to see the town. Suppose you get Useless over there to help you take this car off me and I'll step along. Be back in the morning."

Peter unstrapped the car and one of the young men wonderingly carried it below.

"All right, Gus," Peter laughed. "Have a good time and don't overindulge any."

"Fat chance," Gus said. "They don't put out feed like the *Queen Mary's* over here. Well, so long, and don't take any wooden shillings."

He hopped to the parapet and took off toward the river. Peter went below with the Ambassador.

CHAPTER 9

Fog, Fish and France

The Ambassador and his wife were old friends of the Pepperells; Peter had met them many times in Washington, so he felt very much at home. They were both fascinated by the car and its conveniences. While Peter was proudly displaying these the Ambassador had a transatlantic telephone call put through to the Pepperell home. Within a few minutes Mr. and Mrs. Pepperell and Barbara were all trying to talk at once.

Since Peter's trip and its objective could not be mentioned there was not much to talk about. But everyone said, "Well, how are you?" several times, the Ambassador's wife exchanged a few recipes with Mrs. Pepperell and even Sam the butler was allowed to say, "Well, how are you?" to Peter. Everyone felt quite happy and relieved and everyone commented on the wonders of modern science.

After dinner the Ambassador took Peter into his study for a conference and instructions. He looked behind all the curtains, locked all the doors and sitting close to Peter said in a low voice, "The only information which I may give you is the name of this scientist whom you are to . . . visit. The name — " the Ambassador whispered it, "is Doctor Professor Polopodsky."

Peter repeated it several times until he was sure he would remember it. "That isn't much to go on," he said finally. "Is that all you can tell me?"

"About all," the Ambassador replied. "From here you will proceed to our Embassy in Copenhagen where you will receive further instructions." He opened a wall safe and brought out a small and blurry snapshot. "We have here," he went on, "a photograph of the person in question but I'm afraid it won't do you much good."

About all that Peter could see of the man in the snapshot was a black beard and a pair of thick eyeglasses.

"Since about nine tenths of the men in that country (which of course I cannot name) wear black beards and thick eyeglasses," the Ambassador said, "this is not very useful."

"No, it isn't," Peter agreed. So the Ambassador put the photograph back in the safe and proposed a game of checkers. They played three games, of which Peter won two, and then went to bed.

Next morning the Ambassador waked Peter who wondered why, for the room was as dark as when he went to bed.

"Fog," his host explained, "a real old London pea-souper. Afraid your friend Gus won't show up this morning." Peter went to the window and was sure he would not. The fog was not white or gray, but a thick black curtain. A street light a few feet away was just a dim glow. Even the street noises were muffled.

One London sight that Peter especially wanted to see was the changing of the Guard at Buckingham Palace. So after breakfast the Ambassador suggested that they might try it. He hoped the fog might lift a bit. Peter rode on his shoulder while one of the young men went along as a guide. He had a flashlight and by touching the fronts of the buildings with one hand and the Ambassador's elbow with the other, finally managed to lead them to Buckingham Palace. He could recognize it by the ironwork of the gates.

However, the ironwork of the gates was about all they did see, for the fog was thicker than ever. They heard commands, the stamping of horses' hoofs and the rattle of accouterments, but that was all.

"Well, Peter," the Ambassador laughed, "you didn't see

the changing of the Guard, but at least you *heard* it, that's
something."

Next day the fog was worse, if possible. One of the young
men kept watch on the roof, but there was no sign of Gus.
Sight-seeing was out of the question, so Peter spent most
of the time reading and playing checkers with the Ambassador. Peter politely allowed him to win a game now and
then. The Ambassador's wife saw that the food compartment of the car was replenished and that Peter's laundry
and mending were all done. Mr. Pepperell called on the
transatlantic phone and everyone again said, "Well, how
are you?"

On the third morning, however, Peter waked to see sunshine at the windows. It was thin and sickly, but it *was* sunlight. Immediately after breakfast the young man announced that Gus had returned. Peter rushed up to greet him, but Gus's greeting was far from cheery and his appearance was dreadful. He was excessively thin and bedraggled, his feathers were black with soot.

"Of all the dumps I ever see," he burst out, "this is the last word. Thought Baltimore could be dirty, but at least when we have a fog it's fog, not two thirds soot. As for that Thames River, if there was ever anything to eat in it it must of ben took by the Romans or the Pilgrims or somebody. All's I've had to eat in three days was a hunk of crust. One of these here Limey gulls said it was a scone. Think he meant stone, but they talk so queer you can't tell."

Peter offered to send down to the kitchen for some food, but Gus refused. "No sir," he said, "I've had enough of this place, Pete. Let's get out of here while the sun's still shinin', such as it is. Don't know where we're goin' but any place is bound to be an improvement, as they say. Come on, let's get going."

Peter had the car brought up and strapped on, bade his hosts a hasty farewell and climbed aboard. Gus didn't say good-by to anyone, he just hopped up on the parapet and dove off.

The sunlight, although hazy, was bright enough to see things and Gus finally consented to delay long enough to do a few of the sights. They flew around to the Tower and

watched the Beefeaters making their rounds. "Look like they ought to be in one of them Elks' parades in Baltimore," Gus commented sourly. They sat a while on the Nelson

Column in Trafalgar Square and circled St. Paul's. They paused on a pinnacle at Westminster while Big Ben struck ten.

"Well, I guess we've saw London," Gus said. "Where do we go from here?"

"Copenhagen," Peter answered. Gus brightened up at once. "Now there's a real place," he exclaimed enthusiastically. "Ben hearin' about it fer years. Good clean water and fish by the million." He kicked off and soared at top speed toward the coast.

Soon they burst out over the North Sea. The sky cleared and the sun was brilliant. Below them small fishing boats kicked and foamed in the rough waters. They soared on and on. It was past lunch time when they passed over numerous small islands and reached the coast of Denmark, but still Gus did not slacken his pace. They passed over neat green fields filled with fat cattle and again came to water. At last Gus settled on a sandy beach beside a quiet little bay. Peter hastily unstrapped the car and Gus immediately dove into the clear water. All the time that Peter was eating his lunch Gus dived and splashed and scrubbed, only pausing now and then to snap up a fish. By the time Peter had finished and repacked the car Gus shone with cleanliness and his figure had resumed its old roundness. His disposition had improved too.

All afternoon they passed over sparkling waters and neatly farmed islands. "Looks a lot like Maryland or Delaware," Gus commented contentedly. It was late in the day when they finally sighted Copenhagen. Arrangements for their reception were the same as in London so they were soon able to locate the Embassy.

Gus could hardly wait for the car to be unstrapped. "Now this is a town I really like the looks of," he said happily. "Clean and neat and people eating all over the place. All them squares full of people eating and restaurants right on the edge of the water. I'll do fine here. See you in the morning, Pete." He flew eagerly off toward the harbor.

The Ambassador and his wife were most pleasant and charming. They had a beautiful dinner that evening with a great many dishes which were unfamiliar to Peter, but all of which he enjoyed. After dinner they retired to the study and the Ambassador went through the usual routine of locking the doors and drawing the curtains. Then he drew close to Peter and whispered in his ear, "The country to which you are going is Zargonia."

"You don't say so," Peter said. "I've never heard of it."

The Ambassador pointed it out on a map. "My, it's awfully small, isn't it?" Peter commented.

"Small, but terribly important at the moment," the Ambassador smiled. "You will proceed next to our Embassy in Paris, where you will receive further instruction."

"All right," Peter said, "we'll start in the morning. Do you play checkers?"

He did, but even worse than the Ambassador in London.

Peter tried hard to lose at least one game for the sake of politeness, but it was quite impossible and he was forced to win them all.

Next morning Gus arrived bright and early, filled with good spirits and good food. They started promptly after breakfast, although their hosts begged them to stay longer.

"Now this here is what I call a real place," Gus burst out as they soared over the market place. "Best fish I ever tasted and these here Daners certainly know how to eat. Have any of them smoggersbrods, or whatever they call them, at the Embassy?"

"Yes indeed," Peter answered, "aren't they wonderful?"

"*I'll* say," Gus enthused. "Them restaurants along the shore there serve the best there is. Picked me up plenty of them."

They sailed about the city, admiring the beautiful buildings, the clean squares and parks, the busy harbor. Finally Gus settled on the spire of the City Hall and asked, "Well Pete, found out anything yet, and where do we go next?"

"All I've found out yet," Peter answered, "is that the Professor's name is Polopodsky and that his country is Zargonia. He has a black beard and wears thick glasses."

"That's a big help," Gus snorted. "Now all's we've got to do, I suppose, is to find this here Zargonia and go around yelling 'Call for Mr. Polopodsky,' until he shows up."

"We're to go to Paris now," Peter said. "Maybe we'll learn something more helpful there."

"We better," said Gus as he took off. "Otherwise I'm goin' to come back and settle down here in Copenhagen."

All morning they flew over glistening waters and green islands, over the flat farms of Schleswig-Holstein and on over Holland. They went out of their way to have a look at Amsterdam and Rotterdam, crossed the Rhine and went on over Belgium. Peter told Gus all that he could remember of the geography and history of the places they saw, which was greatly appreciated. It was sunset when they crossed the French border, so they spent the night on a small pond on a beautiful old estate.

They were off promptly in the morning and soon arrived over Paris, where they easily located the Embassy. As soon as Gus was relieved of the car he went off to see the town, while Peter was taken below by the two young men who had met them.

"I'm terribly sorry," one of them said, "but the Ambassador has not arrived yet. He and his wife were visiting in the suburbs last night and today there is a railroad strike. I planned to send the car for them, but the Chauffeurs Union is having a strike. I would have driven out myself but there is a Police strike, so the traffic is all snarled up. I'd never get through."

"That's too bad," Peter said, "perhaps I'd better speak to him on the telephone."

"That would be fine," the young man sighed, "except that the telephone operators are out on strike as well as the telegraphers."

So they played checkers the rest of the day. The young man played better than either of the Ambassadors, but Peter won most of the games. About dinner time the Ambassador and his wife arrived in a jeep which they had borrowed. They were both tired and exasperated and the Ambassador's wife had to get dinner, because the Cooks and Housemaids Union was on strike.

After dinner the Ambassador took Peter into his study for instructions. Since there were no servants in the house he didn't have to lock the doors or draw the curtains. He brought out a map of Zargonia and showed Peter the lake and the island where the castle stood. He also produced some photographs of the castle. "As far as we can tell," he said, "the Professor's laboratory and living quarters are in this north tower. Lights are often seen there late at night. That's about all we can do for you."

"That's about all we need," Peter said, "— except for one thing. I'd like to find out if there are any sea gulls on this lake and around the castle. It's quite important."

"By George it is, isn't it?" the Ambassador cried. "No one thought of that." He pressed a button and when one of the young men arrived said, "Go out and round up Sokoloff at once."

Then he asked Peter if he played checkers. They played checkers all evening and Peter won nine games to the Ambassador's one. It was past eleven before the young man returned, bringing with him a most unattractive person. He had a bristly black beard, thick glasses, and looked not unlike the photograph of Professor Polopodsky.

"Sokoloff," the Ambassador said, "we want to know just one thing. This lake we have talked of before; are there any sea gulls there?"

"Monsieur," Sokoloff answered, "of these what you call sigguls there are surely a great many. Many times I have been there and always is sigguls; sigguls on the water, sigguls in the air, on the roof even of the castle sit always sigguls."

He looked at his watch and grinned. "You are indeed fortunate, Monsieur Ambassadeur, to be in time. In just forty-five minutes from now our Spies Union is calling a strike. After twelve o'clock there would have been no information."

The Ambassador tossed Sokoloff a package of cigarettes and a pair of nylon stockings and the young man took him away.

"That's fine," Peter exclaimed. "If there are a lot of sea gulls there no one will ever notice Gus. I guess we'd better go to bed now."

CHAPTER 10

The Professor

Gus returned early next morning in a moderately good humor. "This here Seine River," he laughed, "is a worse joke than the Thames, when it comes to fish. The dopey thing about it is that both banks are lined up with men fishin' and one of these here French gulls tells me there ain't ben a fish seen in the river for a hundred years."

"I guess they just like to fish," Peter said, as the Ambassador helped him strap on the car.

"Reckon so," Gus grunted, "but there certainly ain't much profit in it. I made out pretty good though. Lots of cafes and picnickers in these here parks and they leave a lot of stuff around. Swell cooks too, had some French pastry near as good as the *Queen Mary's*."

Peter bade the Ambassador and his wife good-by, Gus said "Grawk," and they set off to see the sights of Paris. Gus perched a while on the topmost tip of the Eiffel Tower, where they had a splendid view of all the city and the surrounding country.

"Real pretty town," Gus commented. "Laid out good, sort of like Washington. Lots of parks and trees and stuff. Pity there's so many French people though."

They flew up and down the great avenues while Peter explained the various buildings and monuments to Gus. They swooped through the Arc de Triomphe, they sat a while on the Vendome Column. They saw the Opera, the Louvre and Napoleon's Tomb. They flew out to Versailles to admire the beautiful grounds and the gorgeous fountains. Finally they flew back and Gus came to rest beside one of the gargoyles, high up among the towers of Notre Dame.

"Well, Pete," he said. "I guess we've saw Paris. Where next?"

Peter got out a map and they located the country of Zargonia and the lake which was their goal.

"Quite a step," Gus commented. "Might's well get goin'."

All morning they flew over the neat farms of France, laid out in long strips of green, yellow and brown. About noon they crossed the Rhine and were over the Black Forest of Germany.

"Don't see why they call it black," Gus grunted, "looks plain green to me. Jest one of them dumb furrin ideas I guess."

Far off to the south they could see the towering peaks of the Swiss Alps gleaming white in the clear sunshine. Early in the afternoon they swooped down to the beautiful blue waters of Lake Constance, where Gus indulged in a hearty meal of fish. They did not linger long, for he wanted to make the castle before nightfall.

It was almost nightfall when they crossed the border of Zargonia. The country was so small that it took only a short time to locate the lake. It was exactly as the maps and photographs had shown; a fair-sized lake with a small round island in its center. Occupying most of the island was an old, ivy-covered castle.

All around the shores could be seen raw trenches, gun emplacements, tanks, trucks, jeeps and all the evidences of the guarding Zargonian army. Overhead was the constant hum and crisscrossing of planes. Because of these Gus flew low over the trenches. They could see the unsuspecting troops gathered about their campfires and smell the odors of the evening meal.

Gus swept out over the lake and circled the castle a few times. Finally he lighted on the parapet of the north tower. There were many gulls roosting on the roofs so their arrival went unnoticed. The sun was just setting over the mountains to the west. The castle seemed completely quiet, almost deserted. Down in a tiny garden they could see a bent old man puttering among the vegetables. From one or two chimneys rose lazy drifts of smoke laden with the pleasant odors of cooking.

"Well here we are," Gus announced quietly, "all safe and sound, as they say. Now Pete, what I figger is this. That window right below us is the one they told you was this here Professor's study. Lucky it's open. Landing on the window sill might be risky, so we'd better land here. You can climb down this ivy easy as not and have time for a good look around before you go in. What do you think?"

"I think it sounds very sensible," Peter answered. "Let's go eat our supper."

They flew off a few miles to a quiet little pond where Gus had himself a good meal of fish. Peter also ate a stout dinner, for there was no knowing when he would have his next, if any. Then they napped until it was thoroughly dark.

As darkness fell the sky became crisscrossed with the blue-white beams of searchlights. As Gus winged in over the lake they were almost blinded by the glare, but no one paid any attention to this lone gull flapping his way toward

the castle. A dim light in the Professor's study revealed no sign of occupants.

"Still eatin' his dinner," Gus guessed as he landed gently on the parapet. "Looks like a good chance right now."

Peter hopped out of the car, strapped on his tiny sword, and stuffed a flashlight and a few chocolate bars into his pockets. His heart was thumping rather loudly, but he managed to bid Gus a cheery good-by as he grasped the ivy and lowered himself over the edge. The ivy was thick and strong. It made a perfect ladder down to the window sill.

Peering in the open window Peter saw a fair-sized, lamp-lit room. There were a large desk, several comfortable chairs and a fireplace. One wall was lined with bookshelves. The only strange thing was a large and gaudy American pinball machine standing against the farthest wall. Peter looked up at Gus, who was leaning intently over the parapet.

"I'm going in now, Gus," he called softly.

"O.K., Pete," Gus answered. "Watch your step. I'll stick around. All's you have to do is flash your flashlight or wave your handkerchief and I'll be right there. Good luck."

Peter swung himself down by the curtain. The book-shelves seemed the best hiding place so he climbed up there. The books were old and dusty and unevenly ar-ranged. Behind them was considerable space, while the disorderly gaps afforded excellent peep views of the whole room. Exploring around on the fourth shelf Peter dis-covered a small safe set in the wall. The books in front of it were not dusty, nor was the safe itself. It seemed to have been recently used.

At this moment the door opened and a man entered the study. Obviously it was Dr. Professor Polopodsky. There were the same bushy hair, the black bristly beard and thick eyeglasses of the photograph which the Ambassador in London had produced.

The Professor was picking his teeth and humming contentedly. He walked over to the bookshelves, reached up to the fourth shelf and removed the books from in front of the safe. Peter shrank back and remained quietly within six inches of the groping hand that now twiddled the knob of the safe. The door opened, the hand reached in and carefully took out two tiny cardboard boxes. These the Professor placed gently on the desk, then seated himself.

Squeezing between two books Peter could look directly down on the desk. He saw the Professor open the two boxes. Each contained a small capsule resting in a nest of cotton. One capsule was quite filled with a coarse granular substance, the other seemed to contain only one grain.

Peter's heart beat loudly as he realized that here, only a few feet away, was the dread secret which had half the nations of the world in a dither.

Professor Polopodsky took the full capsule from its box and tossed it carelessly on the desk. It rolled closer and closer to the edge, while Peter grew cold and held his breath. It rolled off the desk and bounced harmlessly on the floor!

"Damn," said the Professor. He picked up the capsule and put it on the desk again. "Lucky it wasn't the real stuff," he chuckled.

Peter was astonished to note that he spoke in perfectly good English, or rather American, and rather tough American at that!

The Professor carefully closed the box containing the almost empty capsule and gently replaced it in the safe.

There was a knock at the door and an ancient butler ushered in an officer, resplendent in the gaudy uniform of the Zargonian army. The officer seemed terrified, his face was pasty white and little beads of perspiration shone on his forehead. His eyes remained fixed on the capsule which the Professor now held in his hand. The Professor barked a question in Zargonian to which the officer hastily answered "Jah! Jah! Jah!" He clapped his hands and a soldier entered, carrying a heavy bag which he placed on the desk.

From this Professor Polopodsky lifted roll after roll of shining gold coins. He stacked them up and counted them carefully.

"Good," he finally muttered under his breath, in English. "Fifty t'ousand bucks." The soldier removed the bag and withdrew.

The Professor swept the gold into a drawer of the desk and asked another question, upon which the officer again clapped his hands. At once a man in civilian clothes entered. He was a tough-looking individual with a broken nose and a cigarette dangling from his lip.

Polopodsky stared at him fixedly for a moment and then spoke, this time in very broken English. "You are the mechanic Americaine, who perhaps can the machine to fix, yes? She is — how you call it? — bust. It make me very sad, for she is my only amuse."

The American grinned and went over to the machine.
"If I can't fix it," he announced, "nobody can. Fixin' these
was my racket back in the States — fixin' them so they
always lost." He drew a screwdriver and a pair of pliers
from his pocket and went to work.

The officer, mopping his damp forehead, backed out and
closed the door, his eyes all the while fixed on the capsule

with which the Professor absently toyed. There was a long silence, while the American worked busily at the machine. Outside there was the never-ending buzz of the patrolling planes and the occasional sleepy "quark" of a roosting gull.

Suddenly Professor Polopodsky called, "Well, Lumps, how're you coming?"

The other man spun around as though shot. His jaw dropped and the pliers fell from his hand. "Whaddaya mean Lumps — who are — how'd you —?" he gasped.

Professor Polopodsky roared with laughter. "Lumps Gallagher," he chortled, between spasms. "My old pal from Chicago. What're you doing in this Gawd forsaken dump?"

To Peter's amazement, and the still greater astonishment of Lumps, Dr. Professor Polopodsky reached up and swept off the black wig, the thick glasses and the bristly beard. He was revealed as a swarthy, hard-faced young man of about thirty!

"Fisheye Jones!" gasped Lumps. "Fisheye Jones! Well whaddaya know!"

The two men shook hands and pounded each other on the back, all the while shouting questions and exclaiming, "Whaddaya know about that?"

Fisheye jerked a bell pull. The old butler brought two enormous pitchers of beer. Lumps finally managed to ask, "But what's about this Professor Pollpolly, or whatever's his name?"

"Dr. Professor Polopodsky?" Fisheye laughed. "I'm him."

CHAPTER 11

The Tale of Fisheye

After the two men had quieted down a bit and absorbed some of the beer Lumps Gallagher said, "Come on now, Fisheye; tell. What's the racket and how come you're here instead of the Loop, Chicago, Ill?"

Fisheye put his feet on the desk, lit another cigarette and said, "Well it's the best racket ever, Lumps, and a long story, but I'll make it short. Here goes.

"You remember maybe, my folks out in Chicago? They come from this Zargonia. The name was Jonowkowski, but I took Jones — it was easier. The old folks always talked Zargonian at home so of course I talk it as good as a native. Well, when the war come I got drafted."

"So did I," Lumps said wryly, "but I thought you was too smart."

"I could of been," Fisheye continued, "but I'd got in a little misunderstanding with the police in Chicago, so I thought maybe some foreign travel on Uncle Sam might be good for my health. I won't bother you with the story of what a war hero I was, but along toward the end of it my outfit ends up here, right in Zargonia. Knowing the language like I did I had myself a soft job as a inter- preter."

"You would," Lumps laughed.

"I would," Fisheye agreed and went on, "but when the war was over I got fed up with all this brushing your teeth and saluting and stuff so I sort of resigned."

"You went over the hill?" asked Lumps. "Deserted?"

"If you want to put it crude like that — yes. How did you get out?"

"Same way," Lumps admitted.

"Well I had myself to look out for and I saw this pinball machine in a U.S.O. hut and I got an idea. So I sort of lend-leased it to myself. Then there was a jeep that nobody seemed to be using so I put the marble bouncer in the back seat and I made a little tour of Zargonia.

"It was a good racket. Chicken-feed, of course, but not too bad. You see these Zargonians like to gamble and they'd never seen one of these machines and they went nuts over it. I toured around to the fair days and the feast days and the cafés and the night clubs and always had a line-up waiting to risk their dough. They didn't have an awful lot, but what they had I got."

"You would," grunted Lumps.

"I would," Fisheye agreed. He had another glass of beer and went on.

"Well, the M.P.'s were sort of looking for me, so one evening when I happened to be passing this lake it looks like a good spot for a little quiet rest. I park the jeep in a patch of woods, get a guy to row me and the machine out here to the island and set up shop in the kitchen of the castle. Of course these servants was as nuts about the game as all the rest of them and in a little while I'd had a good dinner and took in their last six months' wages. Then the boss, this old Prof. Polopodsky comes down to the kitchen for something and sees the machine. He's as nutty about it as any of them — only more so.

"He had it brought up here to his study and we play the thing all night, not for money of course, just for fun. We played it for a week. Well, it suited me fine. I wanted to be out of circulation for a while and this dump certainly is out of circulation. Good food and good beer and lots of service. All day the old guy would be working in his laboratory while I'd eat and sleep and fish off the dock. Then all night we'd play pinball.

"He was a queer old geezer, sort of a *ree*cluse like they call 'em. Didn't have any friends or relations, never went anywhere and no one ever come here. He took a big shine to me, acted like I was his own son.

"He got so friendly he finally told me all about this secret thing he was working on. Seems he'd invented something about a million times more powerful than the atom bomb. He'd been working at it most of his life and had only managed to make three grains, about like grains of sugar. Kept 'em in a capsule right here in this wall safe.

"Well, I had a nice easy summer, not taking in any money, but not putting out any either. Then all of a sudden the old man died."

Lumps made a strange sound, half chuckle and half snort.

"No, I hadn't nothing to do with it," Fisheye said indignantly, "I don't go for that sort of thing. He died perfectly natural, old age or something. Having no friends or relatives or anything the servants just planted him down in the family chapel with all the honors.

"Then all of a sudden I got an idea. The Real Big Idea. I get the servants all together and tell 'em, 'Look; from now on *I'm* Doctor Professor Polopodsky. You just obey orders and keep your traps shut and you'll all get a wheelbarrow full of dough.' Well times were tough around here and they had a soft job; all they could eat, easy work, free beer, big wages. So they decide to co-operate.

"I fix myself this wig and beard, put on the old man's specs and go to see the Zargonian Minister of Defense. They'd all heard how the Prof. was a great scientific genius and a little queer in the head, but none of 'em had ever seen him, so I got away with it easy. They agree to have a test of this new super-duper explosive. We tried it — two grains out of the three — out in the middle of the Gobi Desert. It was quite a bang."

"You mean that earthquake last October?" Lumps asked.

"Earthquake my eye!" laughed Fisheye. "That was two grains of the Polopodsky extra special. The old boy certainly had the stuff. It convinced the Zargonian Government all right and every other Government in the world. They soon found out it wasn't any earthquake and they're all scared to death.

"Well, I come right back here and do the queer old Professor act. I send for the President of Zargonia and the Defense Minister, and they come running. I tell them I can turn out this stuff by the bushel, *but* if they don't play ball or if I'm bothered by anybody I'll just slam a handful on the floor and Good-by Zargonia. To say nothin' of Good-by Europe and most of Asia. They was sweating like porcupines and ready to kiss my foot.

"*Then* I tell them, and of course this was the whole point of the racket, that just to keep me happy-like and contented I'll accept fifty thousand smackers in gold, coin of the realm, on the first of every month. They agree so quick I wished I'd made it a hundred. That General that brought you here tonight also brought the rent."

He pulled open the desk drawer and exhibited the gold coins. Lumps stared at them goggle-eyed.

"You always had big ideas, Fisheye," he said enviously, "but this is the biggest yet. How long's this been going on?"

"Ten months," Fisheye answered contentedly, "and ten times fifty thousand is five hundred thousand, as my teacher told me. They give me an extra two months allowance for a Christmas bonus so the total is six hundred thousand, as of the close of business today. When it's an even million I'm goin' back to Chicago and buy the City Hall."

"I always knew you was a genius," Lumps said, "but not this much of a one. How did I happen to come in on this?"

"Just pure accident," Fisheye replied. "Just an accident and a lucky one for the both of us. You see I been paying these servants a big lump of cash every month. Then they come right up and play the pinball machine and I get it all back, so the whole layout don't cost me a cent. Last week the machine broke down, so I tell this Zargonian General to fetch me a good repair man — or else. He finds you, how or where I don't know, but it was sure good luck."

"How or where," Lumps said, "don't matter. I been doin' a lot of things since I went over the hill — I mean resigned. But it *was* lucky."

"The luckiest thing about it is this," Fisheye said. "Gettin' this load of gold back to the States is goin' to be quite a big job, too much for me to handle alone. I can finagle the officials and all that end, but I *got* to have a partner. And here Fate or something brings me my old pal Lumps Gallagher to be it. What do you say, Lumps, is it partners?"

Lumps merely rose and extended his hand. "What's my end?" he asked.

"I'll cut you in for ten per cent," was the answer. "That'll net you a hundred grand — and no income tax."

They shook hands and had some more beer. Fisheye absently began bouncing the capsule on the desk. Each time he did so Lumps cringed. His partner laughed. "Nothin' in this one but sugar," he said, "right out of the old sugar bowl. I only use this one for impressing the military."

He went to the wall safe, gently extracted the other tiny box and opened it. "There's the real McCoy," he exclaimed.

Lumps, fascinated, gazed at the capsule and its one tiny white grain. "Wot a meal ticket," he breathed, "wot a meal ticket! Put it away, Fish, it makes me noivous."

Fisheye closed both boxes and put them gently in the safe. He closed the door, twirled the knob and replaced the books. Then the two had some more beer and went off to bed.

Peter, worn out with excitement, ate a chocolate bar and curled up behind the books to go to sleep. It was maddening to know that here, within two feet, was the fateful capsule which they had come so far to secure. To know that Gus was undoubtedly waiting faithfully on the parapet, ready to carry him away — if he had it. Yet the capsule was as unobtainable as though they were still in London.

The Rockets' Red Glare

It was so dark behind the books that Peter slept quite late.
When he woke the study was flooded with sunshine and
quite deserted. The whole castle seemed quiet, so he ven-
tured forth, swung over to the window sill and stepped
out. Far below he could see the bent old man puttering
in the garden. He was also relieved to see Fisheye and
Lumps seated on a tiny dock fishing. They seemed to be
talking animatedly, no doubt planning ways and means of
getting their gold hoard back to the States.

Peter waved his handkerchief and almost at once Gus

settled beside him. "Well, Pete, how's it going?" he greeted. Breathlessly Peter poured out the whole tale of the bogus Professor, interrupted now and then by Gus's "Well ain't that somethin'."

When he had finished Gus said, "Well, we sure are close to it. Gettin' warm, as they say. If it only wasn't for that safe it'd be duck soup. Too bad your old man didn't teach you safe crackin'."

"It is," Peter agreed. "The only plan I can think of is for me to stay hidden behind the books and watch. Perhaps when Professor — I mean Fisheye — opens it again I can learn the combination."

"He may not open it again for a week, or a month maybe, Gus ruminated. "Goin' to be a teejus wait, but it seems to be the only answer. But whenever I see them two fishin' I'll know it's safe to come up here for a visit. Safe for me to get a bite to eat too. Rest of the time I'll be right up there on the cornish or cruisin' around keepin' an eye on things."

Peter extracted a blanket from the car, filled a "Thermos" bottle with water and got out some bread and cheese; chocolate bars had begun to pall. These were all carried in and settled behind the books.

The pair on the dock now seemed to have finished their fishing, so Gus said good-by and soared off to do a bit of fishing on his own account. Peter climbed back behind the books and settled down for the long wait.

A little before noon Fisheye came in and removed the gold from the desk drawer. He put it in a handbag and carried it away, doubtless to add to his main hoard. Peter hoped he might open the safe but he didn't go near it.

After lunch the two came into the study and spent the afternoon playing pinball and drinking beer. They talked a great deal about the old days in Chicago and about their schemes for transporting their ill-gotten gains back to the States. Peter couldn't understand most of their jargon but he listened carefully, still hoping the safe might be opened. It was not, and eventually the pair went down to dinner.

The evening was a repetition of the afternoon; pinball, talk and beer, a great deal of the latter. Peter was stiff and cramped and sleepy. It was a relief when the two finally staggered off to bed, considerably the worse for beer. Peter snuggled down in his blanket and was asleep almost before they were out of the room.

Much later he was wakened by a slight sound. There was a bright moon outside which, combined with the glow of the searchlights, made a fair light in the study. Peter's hair prickled as he heard heavy breathing and the sliding of the books in front of the safe. Slipping from his blanket and peering out he recognized the ugly head of Lumps Gallagher silhouetted against the window. Lumps was muttering to himself.

"Smart guy, Fisheye," he mumbled, "very smart. Only he forgets his old pal Lumps is the best little old can opener in Illinois. Lil' old can like this is kids' play. Ideer of offerin' a measly hundred grand to an old pal. It's insultin'. All's I need is this little meal ticket and he can keep his hundred grand. Lot of good it'll do him when these Spigs string him up an' old Lumps is sitting pretty with this super-duper capsull and blackmailin' the whole world. I'll make his million look like a penny bank."

The books had been removed and Lumps was fumbling with the knob of the safe. Holding his breath Peter unsheathed his tiny sword and moved closer to the hairy wrist. Lumps's beery breath was almost overpowering. Slightly drunk though he might be, the thug knew his work. Peter could hear the tumblers of the lock sliding and clicking obediently. Then suddenly the door of the little safe

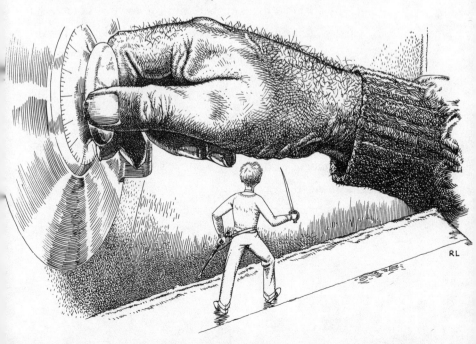

swung open and the huge hand reached in and began to paw around.

Now was the moment! Peter drew a long breath, straightened his arm and plunged the sword into the wrist, just below the base of the thumb. At the same instant he sharply squeezed the sword hilt. For one awful moment of doubt nothing happened.

The hand remained motionless. Then it slowly grew limp and slid with steadily increasing speed out of the safe and down over the edge of the shelf. There was a heavy thump as Lumps's unconscious body crashed to the floor.

Leaping into the safe Peter snatched open the two tiny boxes and carefully slid the two capsules into his side pockets. He stepped out, caught the curtain and swung easily to the window sill.

It was just in time, for at that moment the door crashed open and Fisheye Jones rushed into the room. In one hand he carried a flashlight, in the other a wicked-looking automatic. As the beam revealed Lumps's sprawled form and the open safe Fisheye uttered a roar of rage.

Peter, on the window ledge, had been frantically blinking his flashlight, now the white gleam of Gus's wings materialized from the darkness as he settled on the ledge. The movement also caught Fisheye's attention. At once he began firing blindly toward the window. Luckily all the shots went wild, one bullet glanced from the stone sill and whined out across the lake.

Peter leaped aboard and Gus, without command, dove
straight down, so straight that Peter, for a second, thought
he had been hit. But a few feet above the ground the broad
wings straightened out, they pulled out of the dive and shot
out across the lake at terrific speed, just skimming the surface of the dark waters. It was a wise maneuver, for Fisheye, now at the window, was firing viciously. But the shots

had roused all the other gulls and the air was now filled with them, so Peter and Gus were soon completely hidden by the wheeling, flapping flock.

The shots too, had startled the Zargonian army. Machine guns started to spit long sprays of tracer bullets in every direction. As Gus swept over the trenches they could see soldiers tumbling over each other to man the guns. Colored signal rockets shot up, the long searchlight fingers probed wildly, the planes made screaming dives. Two of them collided and plunged like flaming meteors into the lake. Gus swerved and banked, shooting swiftly through the tall pine trees. In a few moments they were soaring quietly over the sleeping countryside. Behind them the rattle of machine guns rose to a terrific pitch, then gradually faded away. The glaring searchlights continued to explore the sky.

"Phew," Gus called over his shoulder, "we sure got away in a blaze of glory, as they say. You all right Pete?"

"Yes, I'm fine," Peter answered happily, "and I've got it — the capsule."

"Great work," Gus exulted. "I'll hear about it in the morning. Right now I'm goin' to keep moving. Just as soon put a couple of hundred miles between us and them Zargonian nuts. Better take yourself a nap."

Peter went into the cabin and gently removed the two capsules from his pockets. The dangerous one with its single deadly white grain he wrapped in several handkerchiefs. This he placed in the center of his pillow, carefully rolled it up and tied the bundle with a couple of neckties. The roll just fitted snugly into one of the lockers. Peter breathed a sigh of relief when this delicate operation was completed. The capsule filled with sugar he stuck back in his pocket.

He was too excited to go to sleep at once. He was much smeared with dust and stiff all over from his cramped quarters on the bookshelf. It was luxurious to stretch out on his soft bunk and watch the stars parade past as Gus winged smoothly and swiftly southward. Finally he slept.

CHAPTER 13

The Glory That Wasn't Rome

Gus flew through most of the night, landing sometime before dawn on the waters of a tiny mountain lake. When Peter waked the sun was just peeping above the surrounding pine trees. They were floating peacefully in a small cove. Gus slept soundly.

Peter got out some soap, threw off his pajamas and dived in. The water was icy cold, he shrieked and whooped, splashing toward the shore. Gus woke, yawned and paddled up to the sand. "Be obliged if you'd take off this contraption for a while, Pete," he said. "Ain't had it off sence we left Paris."

Peter quickly unstrapped the car and while Gus splashed and snapped up fish he soaped and scrubbed off all the castle dust. Then he ran up and down in the warm sun until dry. The fresh mountain air and the icy water had made him ravenous, so he built a fire and cooked an enormous breakfast. Gus stretched, ruffled his feathers and preened happily in the sunshine. "Mountain trouts," he yawned contentedly, "almost as good as shads."

They spent the whole morning on the lake shore, resting and relaxing after the strain of the past few days. Peter related last night's adventures. "Sure was a risky business," Gus said gravely. "You done fine, Pete; real quick-witted, as they say. Your old man oughta be proud of you."

"I'm pretty proud of him," Peter replied. "That sword worked perfectly. I'd certainly have been in a mess if it hadn't. I'd have been in a mess, too, if you hadn't been right there. You were wonderful, Gus."

"Aw shucks," Gus said modestly, "all I done was stick around." He chuckled, "Wonder how that Lumps Gallagher's feelin' about now?"

"Father said the drug lasted about twelve hours," Peter said, consulting his watch, "so he's still probably unconscious."

"Will be from now on, if that Fisheye's as tough as he sounds. Fisheye won't last long either," Gus opined, "once them dumb Zargonians learn how they've been done. Oh well! they was a bad lot, the two of them. Good riddance, as they say."

Peter looked over his food supply, now fairly well depleted, filled the water tank, made his bunk and got out a map. Lying in the warm sun he and Gus studied it. Peter roughly figured their present location.

"Don't know about you, Pete," Gus yawned, "but far as I'm concerned I've saw Europe. Course there's the Spinks and the Pyramids, but they're way out of our way and probably ain't half what they're cracked up to be anyway. Personally, I'd just as soon see the docks down to Baltimore."

"That's the way I feel," Peter agreed. "Besides, we ought to get home as soon as we can and tell Father and the Secretary of State. Carrying this awful capsule isn't very restful either."

They studied the map some more. "If we go on south," Peter suggested, "we could see Venice and Florence and Rome. Then we could go down the Mediterranean, pass the Rock of Gibralter, stop at Madeira and then right across the ocean and home."

"Suits me fine," Gus agreed, "couldn't be better." Glancing at the map again he suddenly cried, "What's this here island called Sardinia? That where sardines come from?"

"I think so," Peter said.

"*That's* where we spend the night," Gus announced decisively, "come on, Pete, let's grab a bit of lunch and get going. If there's one thing I like better than shads it's sardines."

They ate a hasty lunch, Peter strapped on the car and they were soon under way, to Gus's cheery whoop of, "Sardines, here we come!"

Shortly after noon they reached the waters of the Adriatic and soared over Venice. "Well, what do you know about that?" Gus marveled. "The streets are all water. Certainly must be a soft job for the Street Cleaning Commissioner."

RL

They circled around and eventually came to rest on the dome of St. Mark's, where they had a fine view of the square.

"Real handsome," Gus admitted, "but it must be an awkward town to live in. Certainly wouldn't be much opening here for gardeners or automobeel salesmen. Got a pretty strong scent to it too."

As they flew south Peter suggested, "Florence is mostly art galleries and they don't look like much from the outside. Let's skip Florence."

"Suits me," Gus agreed. "We've got to see Rome though, I guess. Wouldn't do to get back to Baltimore and tell them iggorant fellers we'd been to Europe and hadn't saw Rome." So they saw Rome.

They saw the Forum, the Circus Maximus and the Pantheon. They flew down the Sacred Way and through the Arch of Titus. They saw the Colosseum and all the other historic sights. Gus was astonished and greatly disappointed by their ruined condition. "Sure are in mighty poor repair," he said. "It's a wonder they wouldn't do somethin' about 'em. People comin' from halfway around the world to see these things and them half tumbled down. It's a gyp game, that's what it is."

He was somewhat appeased by the better preserved state of the Vatican, where they flew around the great dome of St. Peter's, but did not linger long, being eager to reach Sardinia before nightfall.

They flew out over the deep blue waters of the Tyr-
rhenian Sea and soon saw ahead the hills and mountains of
Sardinia. Some time before sunset Gus landed in a quiet
little bay and eagerly began his fishing. He had no luck, and
tried another cove. Until long after sunset he tried bay after
bay, getting more and more disgusted as each one failed to
produce a single sardine.

"It's another gyp," he declared angrily. "See Rome; and
all's there is is a lot of tumble-down old ruins. Visit Sardinia;
and there ain't a sardine within a hundred miles."

They were late getting started the next morning, for Gus
insisted on trying his luck again, with equal lack of success.
There were plenty of other fish, so he didn't have to go

hungry, but he was in a poor humor and grumbled considerably as they winged down the Mediterranean. However, the balmy air and the brilliant blue of the water slowly mellowed his spirits. He was his old self by the time the sea began to narrow as they approached the Strait. To the north were the brown hills of Spain, to the south gleamed the white cliffs of Africa. Soon, ahead of them, rose the huge bulk of the Rock. As they came nearer the great mass loomed up grandly.

"Well, Gus, at least *this* isn't a disappointment," Peter laughed.

"Nope," Gus admitted, "she looks real handsome — " He broke off with a sudden squawk of rage. "Another gyp," he roared, "there ain't no printing onto it. Ever picture I ever see of it had printing — great big letters right across the front."

"It did, didn't it," Peter agreed. "I guess they must have gotten washed off during the war." Gus merely snorted.

As they swept through the narrow strait and burst out over the Atlantic Gus's spirits rose again. "Well, Pete," he called, "I guess we've saw Europe. Them as wants it can have it. I'll take Baltimore any time." He winged on with new energy toward Madeira.

His spirits rose still higher when that evening in a secluded cove at Madeira they came on a large school of young pilchards. Gus gobbled sardines until he could barely navigate. With some difficulty he paddled to a tiny sand

beach. Peter removed the car and ate his own supper. The sand was warm, the air balmy. In the east the full moon was just rising. They sprawled contentedly on the sand.

"You know Pete?" Gus said languidly. "There's just somethin' different about the Atlantic. All them rivers and lakes and seas over in Europe's got a sort of funny smell to 'em. Not bad, always, just queer. But the Atlantic smells like home to me, even way over here."

They sat a while in silence, watching the ripples burst into stringed jewels of light along the water's edge.

"Gus," Peter said suddenly. "I've been thinking about that capsule. We've got it and nobody else can get it and I don't think we ought to give it to *anyone* — even our own Government. It's just too terrible."

"Ben sort of thinkin' the same thing myself," Gus replied. "Of course I ain't eddicated, but seems to me that ain't a thing anybody ought to be let loose with. What do you say we dunk her right in the middle of the old Atlantic?"

"Do you think we could — safely?" Peter asked.

"Sure we can. Look; here's what I figger. Tomorrow we fly all day, that'll take us just about to the middle. We spend the night on the water and get a good rest. Next morning I'll go up high — higher'n you ever dreamed of. You got a oxygen mask haven't you? Good. I can stand it a long way up without no mask. When I can't go any higher I waggle my wings. Then you chuck her overboard. When you chuck her you give me a kick in the back — then we scoot. And when I scoot, I *scoot*. Be like to take the hair right off your head, better wear your flyin' suit. Time she hits the water we'd oughta be a couple of hundred miles away and close to the water. How's that strike you?"

"It seems fine, Gus," Peter said, "your plans always do. I don't know whether we really ought to destroy this thing, but I *think* we should."

"'Course we should," Gus said stoutly. "Who's got a better right? We got it, didn't we? Come on, let's go to bed."

They left the car off and Peter slept peacefully. Gus was up before dawn to have another go at the sardines, while Peter cooked himself a good breakfast from his now almost vanished larder. They flew all day with a favoring tail wind which helped them make splendid progress. At nightfall Gus judged that they had reached the exact middle of the Atlantic.

The water was calm, except for a slow lulling swell. They spent a quiet, uneventful night.

CHAPTER 14

Operation Dunk

They both ate light breakfasts, for Gus said that high altitudes and full stomachs were a poor combination. Peter donned his flying suit and settled in the chair as Gus took off and began slowly circling. He anxiously scanned the ocean for ships, but none were to be seen. Even when Gus's seemingly leisurely ascent spread out hundreds of square miles of water below them there was still no sign of a ship. He commented on it and Gus called, "Yep, noticed it myself. Real lucky. Luckier for them even, if the old guy's capsull is all it's cracked up to be."

For an hour or more they circled, rising ever higher. The air grew colder, the circle of the horizon spread farther and farther. Peter went into his cabin and removed the rolled-up pillow. He extracted the deadly capsule and placed it gently in his breast pocket. He got out his oxygen mask and returned to the observation seat.

Another half hour passed. Peter's breathing began to grow labored, so he clapped on the oxygen mask. Still Gus continued his effortless, circling ascent. Their height now must be terrific. The blue of the sky had deepened until it seemed almost black. Below, the limitless disc of the sea shone like white glistening aluminum.

Suddenly Gus's wings began to wabble. Peter reached in his pocket and drew out the capsule. His movements were slow and fumbling. A moment he held the dread thing, then threw it out as hard as he could. At the same instant he stamped heavily on Gus's back.

Immediately Gus went into a steep dive toward the west. Once or twice his wings flapped slightly as he banked to catch a new angle. The speed became appalling. Peter was squashed back into the seat as though pressed by a huge invisible hand. The very breath seemed crushed from his lungs. The whisper of the passing air rose to a whine, then to a whistle, then to a shrill scream. Still Gus dived on and on. A dim memory of his words flashed through Peter's brain, "When I scoot, I *scoot!*"

The blue of the sky was now more normal, the sea looked more like sea and less like aluminum. Peter turned his head to look back and the air promptly snatched off his oxygen mask. They must have reached lower altitudes, for he could breathe without it, but he had to keep his mouth closed. He was sure that if he opened it the rushing wind would blow him up like a toy balloon.

It was fifteen minutes, twenty minutes, it must have been half an hour since he had dropped the deadly load, and nothing had happened. He began to wonder if this capsule was a hoax too.

Then, far back on the distant horizon he saw a beautiful pink mushroom slowly grow from the sea. Higher and higher it rose, the top gently spreading out. Above it a small puff of paler pink floated a while, then dissolved. He wanted to call Gus's attention to it but Gus was too busy to be disturbed. His outstretched head, his neck and body were as rigid as carved wood. Only the ever-quivering tips of his wings showed any sign of animation.

The mushroom on the horizon was changing now. Its outlines grew less sharp, its color darker. It lost its form and began drifting away in a shapeless mass. It seemed incredible that this huge disturbance could have occurred so soundlessly. Then Peter realized that it was a hundred or

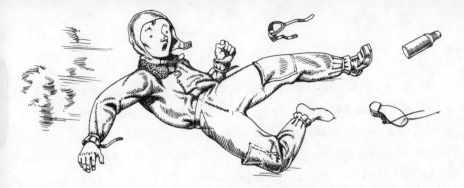

more miles away. It would still be some time before the sound and the blast caught up to them.

It caught up sooner than he had hoped. Above the shrill whine of their own progress there slowly developed a rumbling, roaring, rushing sound. It grew louder and louder. Gus turned his head for one quick look and redoubled his efforts. Across the sea was approaching a dark line of disturbed water.

The blast struck them like the blow of a giant's pillow. One moment they were shooting smoothly, the next Gus was flying end over end. The straps of the car tore loose. *Pete's Ideer* went spinning in one direction, Peter in another. As he fell he caught one glimpse of Gus struggling valiantly, but helpless as a bit of down in the blast of an electric fan.

They were not very high above the water, but to Peter the drop seemed endless. He tried to roll himself into a ball, but didn't quite succeed. He struck the water awkwardly with a terrific splash. He felt a shooting pain in his chest, there was a rushing sound in his ears — then blackness. . . .

The blackness changed to blue and then to pale green.

He realized that he was struggling frantically toward the surface. A moment later he burst out into the sunshine, gulping great gasps of air which burned like fire. His flying suit had retained some air, making it quite buoyant. He rolled over on his back and floated quietly until his breathing became less labored.

A confused sea had been kicked up by the blast. Now lifted high by a wave he saw Gus swimming aimlessly about. At the same moment Gus spied him and skittered slowly over. He spread one wing in the water and maneuvered it under Peter's floating form, making a sort of feathered ramp. Up this Peter managed to crawl, then sprawled out on Gus's broad back.

"You O.K. Pete?" Gus inquired anxiously.

"I think so," Peter answered in a weak voice. "I hit the water awfully hard. It gave me a terrible pain in the chest, but it isn't so bad now. I feel pretty shaky though."

"Sort of groggy myself," Gus admitted. "Man oh man, but didn't we set off a firecracker! That old Perfesser certainly knew his stuff. Glad that little pill's out of the way, though. And to think of you carrying it around in your pocket!"

They were silent for a while, then Gus continued worriedly, "You got to ride piggyback from now on, Pete. Last I see of the car she was half a mile away and goin' strong. Sunk by now I reckon."

"Oh that'll be all right," Peter answered, "I've done it before."

"Not so sure it *will* be all right," Gus pointed out. "You got no food and what's worse you got no water, and we're a long ways from home. What I figger is, we better head for the Bahamas. Got a good wind and we'd oughta make it by tomorrow morning, but you're goin' to be mighty thirsty 'fore then."

With a slightly sinking heart Peter realized that he was already thirsty. What with the shock, the salt water that he had swallowed and the blistering sun he craved a good cool drink intensely. However, he bravely said, "Oh I'll be all right, Gus, besides, we may get a shower."

"Hopin' for that," Gus said. "Doubt we'll hit any 'fore late afternoon, though. Well, we can't do nothin' but try, as they say. Give me five minutes more and I think I can take off. I'll make all the speed I can, just you hang on tight."

With the choppy sea and his own exhaustion Gus had to make several tries before he could get off the water. When he finally succeeded he swung toward the west and soared off at an encouraging clip. There was an excellent tail wind, Gus flew close to the water and Peter could see from the way the waves skimmed past that they were making great speed.

He was encouraged, but far from happy. The wind and the glaring sun made his salt-caked skin burn feverishly. His head ached, he felt dizzy, and the pain in his chest,

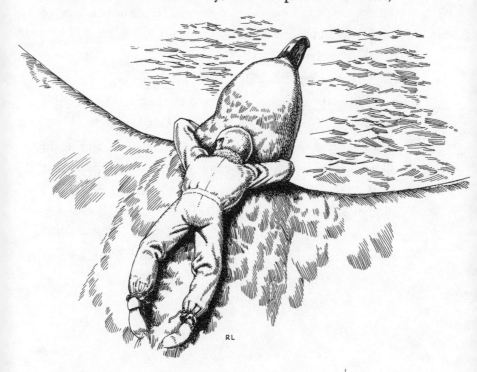

though less, was still nagging. He thought sadly of the comforts of the lost car; the easy chair, the soft bunk — and the water tank! That was the worst blow of all.

Gus, now recovered, was concentrated on his race against thirst. Banking, swerving, constantly feeling the air, he was making tremendous speed. Occasionally he would call back, "How you doin', Pete?" and Peter would doggedly answer, "Fine, Gus, fine." Toward midafternoon Peter blanked out. He never knew whether he went to sleep or fainted.

He was waked by the delicious coolness of falling rain. Gus had at last located a shower and was now slowly circling under the streaming cloud. The rain washed the salt from Peter's parched skin. He turned his face up and let the drops fall into his dry mouth. He made a funnel of his hands and secured several good sips.

"How you doin', Pete?" Gus called.

"Oh, it's wonderful, Gus, I feel much better."

"Well, take one more drink and then let's get goin'. Still a long ways from home, as they say," Gus laughed.

Towards sunset they struck another shower and again Peter drank. He was hungry now, but the water was a great help. As darkness came down the air cooled and Peter's wet clothes became dank and uncomfortable. He felt feverish, with occasional chills. The stars came out and the moon rose. He hooked his arms tightly over Gus's shoulders and fell into an exhausted sleep.

Gus flew steadily on through the night.

CHAPTER 15

Back to Normalcy

Peter was waked by a bright sun. He was lying on soft sand. Turning slightly he realized that he was nestled against Gus's warm, feathery side. One broad wing covered him.

"Well, Pete," Gus asked, feeling the stir, "how you doin'?"

Peter sat up and looked around. They were on the landward edge of a white beach. All around them was soft tropical greenery. Beyond the white sand danced bright blue waves. He could hear the trickle and gurgle of water.

They were beside a clear bubbling spring that sent a tiny stream down to the beach.

"Where are we?" Peter asked vaguely.

"Island of San Salvador," Gus answered, "in the Bahamas. Folks say it's where Columbus landed, but I wouldn't know, not being eddicated. Anyways, it's where *we* landed and that's a lot more important. Got in a few hours ago. How's about a bath?"

Peter, still sleepy, struggled out of his sodden clothes and plunged into the spring. He drank great gulps, his parched skin soaked up the cool fresh water. Gus, chuckling, flew off into the jungle and returned with some strange fruit. Peter didn't know what it was, but it was delicious. He was still stiff and sore and sunburned, but the pain in his chest was almost gone. He felt ever so much better.

"While you was sleeping," Gus said, "I went over to the town, just to see the sights and hear the gossip. Seems there's a great stew about our little explosion. Lot of ships radioed about it. None of 'em sunk, but they got quite a scare. Big tidal wave in Portugal and they expect one here any time. Whole world's tryin' to figger what done it.

"What I was thinkin'," he went on thoughtfully, "is this. Your old man *he's* goin' to know what done it — and they're all goin' to be worried. They ain't heard from you sence we left Paris. Seems to me we oughta get home soon's we can, if you feel up to it."

"I'm fine," Peter answered, "and you're right. We ought to go right away. They'll worry a lot."

He hastily donned his clothes, which had been drying on a bush, ate some more fruit, had another drink of water and hopped aboard. Gus ran a few steps down the beach and they were off again, this time northward.

The warm fresh breeze and the sparkling blue waters refreshed them both. Shortly after noon they reached Florida and made a stop for Peter to have a drink and some more fruit. They hastened on north.

As the sun set they were near Charleston. Gus sought a cove he knew and gorged himself on small tender shrimp. He peeled one or two and offered them to Peter. Peter had never eaten shrimp uncooked, but found these delicious. They rested a while and flew on. Again the moon rose and the stars came out. Peter slept now and then.

The sun was just rising when they swept into Chesapeake Bay and started up the Potomac. It was still early when Gus wearily landed on the Pepperell driveway, beside the front terrace.

Sam, the butler, sweeping the terrace, was slightly startled as the great bird came to rest. But he was galvanized into frantic activity at the sight of Peter stiffly dismounting. The broom dropped with a clatter. They could hear a siren-like bellow as Sam rushed through the house shouting, "Mr. Pepperell — Mrs. Pepperell — Miss Barbara! He's come home — Mr. Peter's come home!"

"Well, Pete," Gus said, "here we are. I'll be gettin' along over to Baltimore. Leave you to the family, as they say. I'll drop around this afternoon." He ran a few steps and took off. Peter stood alone in the drive.

He was not alone long. The house erupted people. Martha, the cook, burst from the kitchen door, Lena, the housemaid, from somewhere else. Sam rushed back from the front door, the knocker rattling a loud tattoo. He was followed by Mr. and Mrs. Pepperell and Barbara in various stages of disarray.

There were hugs and tears, laughter and questions — chatteration beyond measure. They had heard of the great disturbance in the Atlantic — Mr. Pepperell had guessed its cause — they had sat up most of the last night, worrying. Barbara was concerned over Peter's sunburn. Mrs. Pepperell insisted that he be put to bed at once and Dr. Chutney called.

Peter settled things by announcing firmly, "I want breakfast. I want orange juice and hot biscuit and bacon and cocoa — and bacon and biscuit and bacon and cocoa."

It was a wonderful breakfast, one that lasted half the morning. Peter, alternating stuffings of bacon and hot biscuit, told the entire story. Mrs. Pepperell and Barbara gasped and turned pale at times. Mr. Pepperell grew red-faced, pulled his mustache and swelled with pride. Sam retailed everything to the kitchen.

Suddenly Mr. Pepperell leaped up, exclaiming, "I must talk to the Secretary," and dashed for the telephone. When

he returned Peter asked his father if he had done right in disposing of the deadly capsule.

"It was a grave risk," Mr. Pepperell said, "but it was a fine and wise thing to do. You have performed a great service to humanity. The Secretary agrees with me in this. He is coming out this afternoon to thank you in person."

Peter, overladen with breakfast and exhausted by the excitement, agreed to a bath and a nap until lunch time. He had scarcely lain down, however, when Dr. Chutney arrived to look him over. The Doctor took his pulse, his blood pressure and everything else he could think of. He asked a great many questions and was especially interested in the pain in Peter's chest, which was now completely gone. He listened for a long time with his stethoscope, then turned to Mrs. Pepperell and Barbara.

"Considering all he has been through, he is in remarkably good shape," he pronounced. "Sound as a bell. There seems, however, to be a slight disturbance of the sacro-pitulian-phalangic gland. I shall get in touch with Squarosa at once."

After luncheon a great many people arrived. There were two of Peter's Colonel uncles, the Admiral, the Secretary for Defense, the Secretary of State and a great many others. Peter had to tell the whole story all over again. While describing how he had thrown the deadly capsule into the sea he absent-mindedly took the fake capsule from his pocket and slammed it on the floor. Everyone turned pale and one or two ladies screamed. Rather sheepishly Peter said, "It's only sugar. I brought it for Barbara, for a souvenir."

Suddenly there came a sharp explosion from the front lawn. It was followed by another and another at evenly spaced intervals. They all crowded to the windows and beheld Peter's small army drawn up in perfect array. Buck and the Mephitis Old Guards stood rigidly at attention, while the tiny field guns on the flanks barked out their salutes. They continued until twenty-one rounds had been fired.

Peter was wondering at this unusual expenditure of ammunition when Sam loudly announced, *"His excellency, the President of the United States!"*

The President entered briskly, followed by his military aide, who carried a small box. He shook hands all round, then turning to Peter made a short speech. Peter was too ex-

cited to understand most of it, but he did catch one phrase,
" — the highest honor which is in my power to bestow."

The aide then opened the box and the President drew
out a beautiful gold medal. It was suspended from a broad
silk ribbon and was supposed to be hung around the neck,
but as the medal itself was half as tall as Peter, the President was at a loss as to what to do. Barbara solved it by
hanging the medal beside Peter on the back of his chair.
Of course both she and Mrs. Pepperell were weeping, Mr.
Pepperell was pulling his mustache and the two Colonels
were blowing their noses very loudly.

"Gee, I wish Gus were here," Peter said. "He really de-
serves it more than I do."

"He on the turrus," Sam volunteered, "I'll ask him in."

Gus waddled in, hopped up on the arm of Peter's chair
and cried, "Well, Pete, how you doin'?"

"Fine, Gus," Peter laughed happily, "just fine. Look at the
medal the President gave me. It really ought to go to
you though."

"Aw shucks," Gus protested, "I only done the taxiing.
Personally myself, I'd just as soon have a bucket of shads."

An aide brought a message to the Secretary. He glanced
at it and then came over to Peter and Gus.

"This morning," he said, smiling, "we at once notified
the Zargonian Government of the great hoax which had
been perpetrated on them. You will be glad to know that
your friends Fisheye and Lumps Gallagher have been cap-
tured, almost intact, and turned over to the American

Army authorities. They will at once be tried for desertion.

"The Zargonian Ambassador also craves the honor of an audience with you tomorrow in order that he may invest you with the Grand Cross of St. Filbert, the Supreme Exalted Star of Zarg and several other things that I can't make out."

"That's fine," Peter laughed, "perhaps he could bring along a bucket of shad for Gus."

The President departed, to the accompaniment of another twenty-one gun salute. Gus said, "Well Pete, I'm getting along. Don't take any lead medals," and took off for Baltimore. Gradually the other guests thinned out.

Peter went out and complimented Buck on the splendid appearance and performance of the army. Barbara brought out his medal for them to admire and Peter shook hands all round.

The Secretary, the Uncles and the Admiral stayed for dinner. It was a happy occasion. Sam dropped a tray of coffee cups, Mrs. Pepperell kissed the Secretary and Barbara the Admiral. Peter had to tell the entire story all over again and one of the Uncles made a long speech honoring Gus, which was received with cheers. Peter was pretty tired and soon went up to bed.

No sooner was he tucked in, however, than Dr. Chutney appeared. He was accompanied by Dr. Squarosa and Dr. Squarosa was accompanied by two assistants carrying a great deal of apparatus.

The two doctors did all sorts of things with red lights and blue lights, with things that sparked and things that buzzed and things that didn't seem to do anything. Finally Dr. Squarosa polished his glasses and turned to Peter's expectant family.

"You will doubtless remember, Mrs. Pepperell," he said, "my prediction, several years ago, that some unexpected shock or blow might return Peter's sacro-pitulian-phalangic gland to its normal functioning. I can now state positively that his fall into the ocean did just that. From now on his growth will be perfectly normal. In fact, due to this, what we might call holiday, his growth will probably be far more rapid than usual. While I can not guarantee that he will ever attain to six feet two, I can safely say that within a very few years he will reach the normal size for his age."

Mrs. Pepperell and Barbara cried again and everyone said how wonderful it was. All except Peter; he was quite thoughtful.

"I don't know whether it will be so much fun being normal or not," he finally said. "Gus certainly won't like it, or Buck. Well, we'll just have to wait and see."

There was not much use worrying about it, so he went to sleep.

The
FABULOUS
FLIGHT
of
Peter and Gus

R·L

THE LONG

ATLANTIC

NEW YORK

WASHINGTON

NANTUCKET

CHARLESTON

SAN SALVADOR